The Holiday Switch

The Holiday Switch

TIF MARCELO

UNDERLINED

Text copyright © 2021 by Tiffany Johnson
Cover art copyright © 2021 by Jacqueline Li

All rights reserved. Published in the United States by Underlined, an imprint of Random House Children's Books, a division of Penguin Random House LLC, New York.

Underlined is a registered trademark and the colophon is a trademark of Penguin Random House LLC.

Visit us on the Web! GetUnderlined.com

Educators and librarians, for a variety of teaching tools, visit us at RHTeachersLibrarians.com

Library of Congress Cataloging-in-Publication Data is available upon request.
ISBN 978-0-593-37955-4 (trade) — ISBN 978-0-593-37956-1 (ebook)

The text of this book is set in 11-point Adobe Garamond.
Interior design by Ken Crossland

Printed in the United States of America
3rd Printing
First Edition

To Ella and Anna, my sweet girls

TINSEL AND TROPES
A HOLIDAY BOOK BLOG

Title: The Devil's Holiday by Katie Phase
CATEGORY/GENRE: YA PARANORMAL

Are those considered evil always wrong? And are those considered good always right?

I picked *The Devil's Holiday* for its sleek black cover, adorned with horns and mistletoe, but was cautiously optimistic. I wasn't sure how the author was going to pull off what sounded like a huge undertaking. Drawing on the ever-popular house-switch trope à la *The Holiday* (the film), the plot follows a down-on-her-luck demon who is placed on sabbatical and embeds herself with the enemy— angels on Earth—to learn their ways, only to fall in love with, that's right, an angel. Hello, fish-out-of-water, opposites-attract, and forbidden-relationship tropes!

Let's break down the challenges the author had to overcome.

First of all, the comp: *The Holiday*. To this reader, those are huge shoes to fill. The only thing harder would be to comp *Holiday by the Lake*, which I consider, as you all know, the greatest holiday film of all time. Talk about setting yourself up for major expectations!

Second, the cast of paranormal characters. I love paranormal (you can check out all the holiday paranormals I read here), but angel versus demon? How many times has this been done before?

I was skeptical.

Dear blog readers, I finished this book in one day. In less than twenty-four hours, my eyeballs soaked in this almost-four-hundred-page book, complete with bear-shifter side characters and a town so well described I could draw its map. And now I have a book hangover.

Here's the star on the tree (for those newbs, that means *the best thing*, and by the way, here's the glossary so you can keep up): the Devil is the protagonist. In this world, Devil is the hero and Angel is quite the troublemaker. I got to thinking: What if we looked at things and people in a different light? What if what we thought was true . . . wasn't?

Pros: Quick read and immersive setting.

Cons: There were typos: Fifteen total, and sometimes distracting.

Recommended for: Paranormal aficionados, fans of world building, Twihards! And philosophical types—you know who you are.

Rating: 4 stars

Chapter 1

The sound of jingle bells rips me from my computer screen, where I'm reading through my latest blog entry. Heart rocketing to my throat, I click on the Post button, then slam my laptop shut. From where I'm standing next to the waist-high bookshelf, I dive onto the floor and, in a move that would impress Simone Biles herself, land in a perfect cross-legged position next to a stack of donated books on a vintage sled. For effect, I pick up a book and hold it up to my face just as my boss, Ms. Velasco, walks in.

Lou Velasco's expression is like a beacon of light, as it is every morning. She has a genuine, captivating smile on her face; not a strand of her dark, chin-length hair is out of place, and she's wearing the perfect shade of berry lip gloss—hard to nail, mind you, on medium tawny skin, and I should know—that complements her Bookworm Inn polo. Palming a coffee cup that reads FORGET SANTA, WATCH OUT FOR ME in bold red letters, she says, "Good morning, Lila. Early again?"

"I figured I should get started sorting through these books."

3

I steady my shaking voice and resist the temptation to glance at my laptop on the bookshelf. My best friend, Carm, reminds me time and again that my tells are my croaky voice and shifty eyes, so I focus hard on Ms. Velasco's nose and not on my lingering, ever-evolving thoughts on my blog content, which I have to step up for this holiday season.

Because if Ms. Velasco knew how many times I arrived early before my weekend morning shifts or stayed a few minutes after my closing shifts under the guise of voluntarily categorizing books in the gift shop's free library, she would find out that she's harboring a criminal.

Okay, that's a little extra. Not a criminal, but a sneak, an undercover.

"Well, your work shows." She gestures at the shelves behind me—all donated—and the meticulously categorized books that fill them. The Bookworm Inn Free Library was a community service project I started when I was in the eighth grade with one little shelf and a dozen donated books. Five short years later, the library now lines an entire wall of the gift shop.

"Thank you." My face warms, both from the compliment and the fact that my intentions have not been purely altruistic. Some might say I'm trying to cheat the system—in this case, my parents' rules about certain types of internet use—but I attribute it to my entrepreneurial spirit.

Ms. Velasco twists the watch around her wrist. "Looks like ten minutes before we open. And I spy people in the parking lot."

I scramble up and straighten my Bookworm Inn sweater. It's a soothing forest green that's supposed to embody the gorgeous foliage of the Finger Lakes region. That's where fictional characters Leo Marks and Estelle Mendoza grew up and fell in love in the beloved 1996 film *Holiday by the Lake,* based on its namesake novel. The entire movie was filmed in our real town of Holly, New York, and most of its scenes were shot right here, on the Bookworm Inn property, owned and operated by the Velasco family for the last three decades. Holly has become a major tourist destination as a result, and fans of the movie flock here in droves every holiday season, camera-ready, to relive their favorite scenes.

"I'm ready. I'll put this away and open up."

Ms. Velasco nods, and when she turns, I stuff my laptop into my bag. I really need to be more careful. In my two years stealthily blogging behind the adorable, anonymous avatar of a brown-skinned, dark-haired, Santa-hat-wearing girl, this is the first time I've been close to getting caught in the act.

Which is not on any of my to-do lists. Primarily because Ms. Velasco and my mom are best friends, so anything that happens at the Inn will get back to her. Secondly, the Tinsel and Tropes blog, or TnT, is all mine, even if it's a secret . . . and my plan is to keep it that way.

"Do you know what I think?" I glance at the different displays as I approach the front of the store, catching one pair of askew sunglasses and fixing it.

"What's up?" Ms. Velasco flips a switch above the automatic double doors and tests them. Previously, the manual doors created a bottleneck at the entrance. Installing it kept the traffic flowing and is a mitigation effort to lessen germs, and while the increasing crowds finally convinced Ms. Velasco to invest in it, I can proudly declare that it was me who first suggested it.

"That we should attach a louder bell system to the back door. So we can keep track of who's entering the store from the rear." Plus, I'd know exactly when someone walked in. When you work in a gift shop that caters to the holidays, and live in a town that starts its holiday decorating in September and holds out until almost February, it's easy to dismiss the sound of jingle bells. "Remember that time when we caught a customer trying to grab back access to the Inn?"

I half laugh, though the situation wasn't funny at all. A superfan of the movie's lead actor, the debonair Jonah Johanson, was convinced that the Inn had access to the actor's personal information. The woman figured out that the gift shop back entrance connects to the Inn through a passageway and thought it would lead to him.

"You know what? You're right. You're so on it. I'm sure going to miss you and your attention to detail when you leave us for school in the fall." She takes out her phone and thumbs in my suggestion, but her tone carries a sad lilt despite her smile. "How are applications going? Last I heard from your mom, you've been knocking them out."

Mixed emotions flip-flop in my belly. "I got in to my first choice, Syracuse."

Her eyes round into saucers and she raises a hand. "No. Way."

"Way, and in my declared major. Bio," I proclaim, and I slap her palm. But beneath my joy is uncertainty. Syracuse *is* my dream school . . . and while I qualify for a merit-based scholarship, we're still waiting on the financial aid package.

Her expression changes; she brightens like she's having a lightbulb moment. "No way to the second power. My nephew goes to Syracuse, and in fact—" She's interrupted by buzzing, and she slips her phone out of her back pocket. When she checks the screen, it's like someone turned her energy button all the way up.

"Oh my gosh. I have to take this. Do you mind doing the honors of opening, and I'll woman the registers?"

"Glad to." Grabbing my scarf with the Bookworm Inn's logo embroidered at its ends, I wind it around my neck and, on the way out, snatch the information flyers about the movie, my free library, and the Inn itself, including the few cottages that are available for rent.

I take a purposeful step out of the double doors and smile at the approaching, eager tourists. "Welcome to the Bookworm Inn! Home of the famous movie *Holiday by the Lake*."

Yes, it's cheesy. I'm like a Disney World employee, brimming with cheer and good nature. But I believe in Ms. Velasco, and I genuinely love the movie and the book. I've proudly worked here part-time since my sophomore year, and this job is a large part and parcel of how I'm going to get myself to Syracuse next fall.

I square my shoulders and greet the early bird customers by sticking a flyer in each of their hands as they file through the double doors. Yep, I'm going to make it happen. I *have* to make it happen, one hour at a time.

After a speedy two hours of work that included breaking up an argument between two customers over who was next in line for a photo-op next to the famous canoe where Estelle and Leo had their first kiss, I get to do my most favorite thing: organize my library.

Aligning spines, dusting shelves, and finding the rogue out-of-place book. It's like I'm being paid to play.

I'm balancing eight donated books against my chest as I enter from the back entrance of the shop—because who's got time for a second trip—when my foot catches on the carpet. As I stumble, the pile tips, and the hard corner of a travel book pokes me in the eye, blurring my vision. I become the Leaning Tower of Pisa without the cables that keep it somewhat upright. "Holy fruitcake!"

"Whoa there," KC Chang, another senior from my high school—easily detected by the smell of peppermint gum—steadies me. He takes an armful of books from the top of the stack.

"Thanks." I blink back the last of my tears and he comes into view. He's Chinese American with fair skin and black hair with longish bangs swept to the side. And yep, completely against work rules, he's chomping away at gum.

But what gets my attention are the limp and soggy posters under his arm. "Whoa to you. What happened?"

He grimaces. "What do you get when you mix a toddler with an open bottle of water?"

I make a face.

KC and I, who have worked together for a year, agree that we'd take a hundred customers in twenty minutes over any food or drink accident. The gift shop is always packed to the brim with inventory, and one spill requires us to move the displays, which takes up precious time we do not have. Especially during the busy holiday season.

"Yeah. Luckily these are the only victims." He lifts the posters.

"Hi, you two." Ms. Velasco sticks her head out from her office. "Lila, can we chat for a moment?"

"Sure."

When Ms. Velasco ducks away, KC's eyebrows lift. "What's that about?"

"I don't know. I did ask her the other day if I could work

full-time hours during break," I whisper, wiping my hands on my jeans. My winter break lasts from the twenty-second of December until the fifth of January. Every dollar in my bank account brings me one hundred cents closer to Syracuse, and I need to earn as much as I can before I graduate.

"Eeeks, good luck. I actually asked for the same thing too." He winces.

My heart sinks. I didn't think the other seniors in our part-time crew would ask for more hours. "Well, as long as one of us gets it." I lie, because I have worked one more year than KC, so shouldn't I get seniority? Then guilt runs up my spine. If there's any other part-timer who works as hard as I do at the gift shop, it's him. "Wish me luck."

"Luck."

I straighten my clothes as I enter the office. Ms. Velasco is at her desk, typing at the computer—the reservations dashboard is up. This office is central command. It manages all the aspects of the Bookworm Inn Inc., from the gift shop, the inn, and the community at large. When her mother, Lola Mae, as she was known fondly, passed away, Ms. Velasco inherited the Inn and undertook a full rebranding. Not only did she level up our uniforms, change out the gift shop's new floors, and build quaint rental cabins, she also tapped into the movie's fandom. From online private groups to short reels on TikTok, she's on top of the social media game, touting the Inn as one of the most romantic places to visit. And it has paid off; last year, over two hundred thousand people visited the Bookworm Inn.

Watching her is like a masterclass: she's Filipino American like me, fiercely independent, and doing what she loves.

"Come on in and take a seat." She doesn't look my way, though she's grinning while her fingers fly over the mechanical keyboard, with each switch backlit in red. Each stroke makes a satisfying clack like an old-fashioned typewriter. "Were you bringing in another donation?"

"Yes. Mr. Nadal decided to donate his coveted travel books."

"That's generous of him."

"I know. He's changing tactics."

Ms. Velasco sighs.

"I'm just saying, Ms. V."

Mr. Nadal, the proprietor of Holly's only flower shop, Festive Flowers, has a thing for Ms. Velasco. He repeatedly appears at the Inn for no reason whatsoever. He's sent flowers from "Anonymous" (I mean, c'mon) and even fills our donation jar with dollars instead of pennies to get her attention.

I pass the wall of framed family pictures to my right and take a seat in one of the cushioned chairs. Since Ms. Velasco mentioned her nephew earlier, I scour the photos for a possible shot of him. Sure enough, in one, I spot a young boy in between two women, one who looks to be a young Ms. Velasco.

When I look up, Ms. Velasco's grin has given way to her all-business, deadpan expression. "With your mention of college earlier, I realized I owe you an answer about your request to work full-time. I'm sorry that I wasn't able to get back with you earlier—there's a lot going on."

Score. My back straightens. "Yes. Now that I'm eighteen, I can work full-time until school starts back up after New Year, and then increase my weekly hours. My last semester classes aren't so bad, and I have a couple of extra free periods, so I could leave school early."

Ms. Velasco follows the required labor laws for her under-eighteen hires and insists that schoolwork is priority, so all Book-worm Inn high schoolers are considered the super-part-timers, working no more than twelve hours a week. I worked most of these hours on the weekend, so it didn't affect school at all. Ms. Velasco also encourages us to study during our breaks.

"I want to thank you for your enthusiasm and hard work, Lila. You're such an asset to the gift shop." She entwines her fingers; I don't remember the last time she did that—at my first interview, maybe?

My heart hammers in my chest. The silence is ominous. Me and silence, unless I'm writing, is abnormal and suspicious. At home, it usually means one of my three younger siblings is up to no good. At my babysitting jobs, it was a great indication that a child has gone rogue.

My mind jumps back to the last time I got bad news and the silence that preceded it.

"I've got family coming to stay with me for the holiday season," Ms. Velasco says.

"Oh yeah?" I blurt out, somewhat relieved at the innocuous news. "That's great. I thought your family is all the way in California?"

"They are. My older sister has a son. Teddy—that's my nephew I mentioned—is a freshman at Syracuse University. It's a long story, but Teddy's in a predicament and is staying with me until mid-January."

"Okay." What I'm waiting for is how this has anything to do with me. This arrangement sounds like drama. Ms. Velasco has mentioned her family only a handful of times before.

"So I'm in this position—" The jingle bells of the back door ring, snatching her attention.

A man with white hair, who probably wandered in from the parking lot, lingers after stepping in.

Ms. Velasco stands and heads to the office doorway. "Good morning, sir. This is not the entrance. You'll have to go around the building and enter through the automatic double doors."

A mumbled plea follows.

Ms. Velasco sighs. "Sure, sure, just this one time."

The man is followed by his shuffling family, literally at his heels, as if the cold shoved them in. A myriad of voices verbalize relief from the chill. Then comes the gasp—they've probably discovered all the signed *Holiday by the Lake* memorabilia on the hallway walls. Another thing that elevated the gift shop: the movie props that Ms. Velasco managed to bring in.

When she finally sits back down, she whispers, "Newbs."

We both giggle.

We can tell who's new to the Inn. They murmur excitedly at the film memorabilia, shoved into every corner and hanging on every available hook from the ceiling. Like the empty popcorn tub used in the scene of Leo and Estelle's first date, when they reached for the same kernel of popcorn. The vintage lighter Leo's grandfather gave him when he died, which he used to light the bonfire when they snuck out overnight. Estelle's pager, from which she received that pivotal message of the final twist in the movie.

"What do you think they're going to buy?" I ask. At Ms. Velasco's confused expression, I add, "It's a little game we gift shop workers play. It helps pass the time."

Ms. Velasco taps her chin. "I'll bet, with how eager they were, that they're going to buy a magnet and a sweatshirt each?"

"I'll raise you a thimble and a shot glass."

We both laugh; then Ms. Velasco's smile slips. She stares at me with a remorseful expression.

Dread rises up inside me. "You were going to talk to me about something?"

"Yes. Teddy applied for a part-time seasonal position here, before you sent your email."

"Oh." The shock of it leaves me speechless. I was fully prepared to give up my hours for KC, but not for this . . . Teddy. And no, they aren't my hours to give away, but the Inn is like my second home.

My brain undertakes the mental gymnastics to subtract my anticipated gift shop earnings from my bank account.

"I'm sorry, Lila."

"No. I get it. I understand, but if there's a chance here and there for extra hours, I'll take it." I force a smile and grit my teeth. Only the second half of that statement is true, but Ms. Velasco has always been kind, and she taught me everything I know about retail. She suffered through the first days when I had no idea how to talk to customers; she broke me out of my shell. I'll just have to make up the hours somehow with babysitting.

"Great. Thank you for understanding. Speaking of, Teddy is on his way here to drop off some of his stuff before he goes back for his last week of school." Her face lifts as another set of jingle bells rings out.

"Ah. Here he is." She stands.

A guy walks into the office. He's wearing a hoodie and comfy baggy knit pants with pristine white shoes. His skin is golden brown, and he has lush, wavy dark brown hair, which he pushes back with a hand. Tiny diamonds stud his earlobes.

My jaw slackens. *Oh. My.*

Teddy is *not* the little boy in the picture on Ms. Velasco's wall. Far from it; if I passed him on the street, Teddy would *definitely* turn my head. First, because he's Filipino, and there aren't many Filipino people in Holly. Second, he's cute. Cute in this brooding way that book boyfriends are often described, with prominent dark eyebrows and steely brown eyes.

He sets a duffel bag at his feet, and the clinking of several carabiners snapped into one of the straps momentarily catches my attention.

Ms. Velasco hugs him. "Anak. You look good." She squeezes his shoulders like she's trying to take him in. (I know *I* am.) "Wow, muscles."

"Hi, Tita Lou." He dips his head, as if shy.

My brain is still stuck on *muscles.*

"Lila?" Ms. Velasco's voice yanks me back, and it's only then I realize I was staring at Teddy.

"Yes. I'm sorry, I was looking at . . . Yes, that's me, Lila."

One of Teddy's eyebrows lifts, and his lips curl into a grin. The kind of grin that says, *You're interesting, but in a wearing-a-Halloween-costume-in-December* kind of way.

My neck heats, and I inwardly groan. This feels like the world's most awkward meet-cute.

Ms. Velasco half laughs. "Exactly, Teddy, this is Lila Santos. Lila, this is Theodore, or Teddy Rivera, my nephew. You'll be working together. All of us will be working together. It's going to be such a special few weeks!"

"Great." He nods but doesn't say anything else. In the silence, his expression shifts minutely to what seems like wariness.

I can't tell if he's being sarcastic or indifferent, but it sets off my penchant for hospitality. I want to douse this weirdness like snow over a campfire. "Welcome to the Bookworm Inn, home of *Holiday by the Lake,*" I announce in perfect welcome pitch, like I'm a Holly tour guide, volume eight out of ten. "If you need anything at all, I'm here."

Ms. Velasco claps. "Great. Let me get you to my—I mean, our—cabin. Lila, do you mind manning the fort? We can finish our conversation when I return."

"I don't mind." I release a breath.

Please, go, before I ask him to sign the guest book.

"See you, I guess?" Teddy says, his eyes blank. The guy is obviously not happy to be here. Drama, indeed.

"Yeah, see you."

The two make their way to the back, leaving me in the office with the sound of Bing Crosby piping through the speakers, Teddy's arrival weighing heavily on my mind.

I just gave up my hours to my boss's cute nephew. What the heck am I supposed to do about that?

Chapter 2

SUNDAY, DECEMBER 12

"Whenever you click the refresh button, another angel gets its wings, I swear," my best friend, Carmela Ferreira, gripes behind me. "What are you even waiting on? You're stressing me out."

Sitting at my desk in my bedroom, my eyes trained on my laptop screen, I click the refresh button once more. "Syracuse with my financial aid package. One of my dog-walking clients. A baby-sitting gig. A note informing me that I'm being left an inheritance by a long-lost grandparent."

"*Someone's* been reading too many romance novels. But seriously, you're way too aggressive with that pointer finger. Spill it. You're still upset about the Inn."

"No, I'm not upset." Although the thought of Teddy Rivera and his cocked eyebrow in a Bookworm Inn sweater irks the living nutcracker out of me. What had been empathy for Ms. Velasco and initial acceptance of Teddy has turned, a full twenty-four hours later, into annoyance that I have to replace those hours I expected to work. "Ugh. Yes, okay, I'm upset."

I spin in my chair and face Carm. Despite her earlier declaration, she looks far from stressed. Carm lazily swipes on her iPad while leaning back against my headboard—she's most likely on social media. She's of Portuguese descent, her black hair fluffed around her like a halo, and her legs are crossed in front of her, showing off her mismatched socks. If I turned on a white noise machine, she'd probably fall asleep. I, on the other hand . . .

"Things don't feel like they're coming together."

"It's limbo," Carm says, setting the iPad on her lap. "You remember what Mrs. Emerson said. This last semester is supposed to be a lot about the unknowns. At least you're in with Syracuse."

"Getting accepted isn't the same as going." Again, nervousness rises in my esophagus. Syracuse is my dream school, but it doesn't come with a dream tuition. And there's more to contend with: room and board, and fees, and books.

I also got into my second-choice (and less expensive) school; more schools are pending. I have options. But to be this close, to have worked so hard for something and then lose it because of money?

I hate it.

This time, to calm myself, I spin around and click on a folder on my desktop, then open a file labeled *Books*. An intricate spreadsheet opens, revealing a list of titles labeled as either *Read* or *To be read*, and a sentence or two for each book that will eventually become a review for TnT. Books that I've read are highlighted in yellow, and all that Day-Glo lights me up like the star of Holly's enormous Christmas tree.

Because books. Books are an escape. Books are a reminder that opposites can exist at the same time, both good and bad, positive and negative.

My laptop screen closes, and I jump.

The culprit—Carm.

"Hey!" I say.

She crosses her arms, bangles jangling, and leans back against my desk. We're dressed the same, in long T-shirts over leggings topped by a soft cardi. Looking now, I realize she's wearing *my* cardigan. In our years of spending nights at each other's houses, our closets have become fair game. She probably has about half of my wardrobe at her house, and vice versa.

"You can't click this convo away." She peers at me. "You're doing your best. Have you seen our yearbook? You're in it at least ten times."

"Fourteen." I grin.

She rolls her eyes. "Fourteen. So, whatever happens is going to happen."

"Fine." I heave a breath, hoping to avoid a pity party. I'm not going to discuss dollars and cents with my best friend. Besides, money might not be *her* worry, but getting into RISD, Pratt, or VCUarts is.

We all have something to deal with.

It works, because Carm grins. "Good. Because it's our last holiday break together." She points to a list she hand-lettered and tacked onto the corkboard hanging on my wall, titled *Mission: Holly.* "And you've used work as an excuse twice now to get out of completing anything on our list."

Growing up in a holiday-crazed town didn't mean that we partook in the touristy things. In general, locals avoid downtown as much as possible. Some even leave for the holidays. Holly's like a beach town, except we're on opposite seasons. But last Christmas, while Carm and I were high on candy and good cheer, we decided to complete the Top Ten Things to Do in Holly, New York list from our tourism website by the end of winter break senior year:

1. Kiss on the Bookworm Inn pier
2. Sled down Wonderhill
3. Eat deep-fried marshmallows at Scrooge's Shack
4. Go ice-skating at Prancer's Ice Rink
5. Try apple cider doughnuts at Comet's Cider
6. Make an ornament with Mrs. Claus
7. Decorate cookies at Yule Be Baking
8. Carol while on Holly's Main Street trolley
9. Hot chocolate and chess at the train depot
10. Take a picture with Holly's Santa

Hence, Mission: Holly.

"See this list? We haven't done a single mission," she reminds me.

With Carm's reminder, I deflate. When we made those plans, I didn't anticipate the senior year crunch, and now everything seems to be coming to a head. I'd rather be saving money than spending it on doing touristy things that we all know are overpriced. "Speaking of Mission: Holly . . ."

She waves the notion away, her face scrunched up in a frown. "Nope, nope, don't even! You're not backing out on me. I will not have you lose your Christmas spirit."

I backtrack, her disappointment hitting me as hard as my siblings' when they don't get their way. "No, I'm not backing out. And I'm not losing my Christmas spirit. Everything just feels like it's changing so quickly."

"I mean, because it is? It's not all bad, though. We're almost out of here."

"You sound like my mom." I smile, though it doesn't make me feel better. It's in the air—change. The dip in the temperature yesterday. Work. College. It's as if everything has gone from zero to sixty in the last three months.

"TnT is still the same." She slides a gaze toward the books that are stacked on my desk. One of the perks of running a free library is being able to intercept the books in rotation. "Still racking up the comments. Still reading a million hours a day, which trips me out. Who knew there were so many holiday books? So, not all of it is changing."

Carm is the only person who knows about my blog. And since I don't get to talk about it with anyone but her, I fall back into the topic like a pile of soft snow that's perfect for snow angels. "I want to do something special for my second-year anniversary. There's been an uptick in traffic. I should really take advantage of that."

"When is it? Your blogging anniversary, I mean."

"Second of January."

Her eyes flash with excitement. "Oooh. You could start social media accounts for your blog. That's a good way to branch out."

"Yeah, but won't people want to know who I am at some point?"

"Maybe it's time to let everyone know who you are."

I shake my head. "No. My parents would be furious I kept this from them. Two years I've been blogging—I almost feel like it's too late to say something."

"It's never too late. But"—she presses her lips together, and her eyes glint—"I'll keep thinking. Over our first Mission: Holly excursion."

And we have circled back to her point. Carm is really good at that.

"Hey, Lila?"

I look up to my best friend smiling at me. Not the kind of smile that precedes a joke or a sarcastic remark, but a sincere one. "Yeah?"

"I know lots of things are changing. For me too. But we won't change, okay?"

Relief washes over me. Carm can be so type B; she is my opposite at every given moment, but we balance each other out. It's why, despite how much it's going to pain me to pay for tourist attractions, I will do Mission: Holly.

"Okay," I say.

"Great. Expect a schedule in your inbox by tomorrow." She grins with all her teeth.

I laugh—I take it back. Carm is type B except when it comes to Mission: Holly.

A knock sounds on my door, and a second later Mom steps in. Catherine Santos is wearing comfy clothing: leggings, fluffy socks, and her red-framed glasses that contrast with her dark brown skin. A reindeer antler headband holds back her shoulder-length black hair. And her hands are hiked up on her hips in a pose as she looks off into the distance with a bemused smile on her face . . . because she's wearing the ugliest Christmas sweater on Earth. Sewn-in lights blink red, green, and gold, and fuzzy tinsel trims the sleeves.

I bark out a laugh, and it releases the tension in my chest. Every year she gets a little more extra.

"Whoa." Carm heads to my mother. "That's so ugly it's beautiful."

My mom beams. "It's new. I grabbed it at Ye Old Sweater Shop. It was from last year's stock, and look, since this light's not turning on"—she lifts her left arm and exposes a dim red bulb—"I got it for fifty percent off."

"I love it." Carm's touching all the doodads hanging from the sweater. "Don't you, Lila?"

I approach them to get a better look at the entire ensemble. "Yep. It's so . . . you."

Mom is a pediatric nurse, and she has two sides to her: the serious and the goofy. She can also assess pain levels, and by the way she's currently looking at me, I can tell she's trying to determine mine. I was in a mood when I got home from work yesterday, and she got most of yesterday's interaction with Ms. V and Teddy out of me. "Oh, honey. Still upset about the Inn?"

"Not upset, just disappointed," I admit, because there's no getting around it. While I can keep a secret, I cannot keep my emotions in check.

"Haven't I said not to worry about work? It's your last holiday at home. Enjoy it."

"See?" Carm says with lifted eyebrows.

Mom loops her arms through mine and Carm's. "I know exactly what's going to pep you up. Decorating the tree!"

Carm and I groan at the same time, then break out into laughter. Christmas is no small feat in the Santos household. The switch from Thanksgiving to Christmas is like a slow chugging sleigh pulled by exhausted post–Christmas Eve reindeers. Decorating is the pinnacle.

I don't resist the pull of my mother's arm, and we three attempt to exit my bedroom door at the same time. Unsuccessful, and giggling, we try again and emerge into the hallway, where the rumble and chatter from my family below echoes up the staircase.

I let myself get swept up. Mom and Carm are right—I have to try not to worry.

We're greeted at the great room with an explosion of red, green, and gold and "Frosty the Snowman" playing from the Wi-Fi speakers on the fireplace mantel. The normally dark brown hardwood is covered with decorations, from wreaths to garlands, to rolls of wrapping paper, stockings, and handmade parols. The pièce de résistance, our artificial family tree, stands bare and slightly crooked in the corner of the room.

Almost immediately, my younger sibs start calling out our names.

"Mom, can we eat the candy canes now?"

"Ate Lila, I can't get this ornament on the tree!"

"Ate Carm, what do you want from Santa?"

My ten-year-old twin brothers, Grant and Graham, run up and tug at Carm, who was long ago dubbed a big sister, and bring her toward the pile of stockings to hang on the mantel. Grant's older than Graham by two minutes and twenty-seven seconds and has curly dark hair like Dad, while Grant has feathery and flat hair like Mom's. Carm, who doesn't have patience for the average person, has all the time for my brothers. She's an only child and loves the attention she gets at my house.

Irene, my fourteen-year-old sister, bum-rushes me so the pom-pom of her Santa hat pokes me in the eye. She has a sour expression on her face, a cross between an eye roll and a tongue-sticking-out emoji. Normal, basically. "Mom put me in charge of the Christmas lights. Please help me. I just can't."

Patience is not her virtue.

My dad, Arturo, in the eye of this tornado, is attempting to round everyone up like a Puppy Bowl referee.

We are a brood. The Santos family consists of Mom, Dad, me, Irene, Grant, and Graham. The bottom line is that we are *a lot*, especially while putting up ornaments. It is not a peaceful process, with one person complaining, or a glass ball breaking, or two people fighting at any given time.

But after a couple hours, it's only Carm and me trimming the tree—the rest have lost steam. Dad is at the stove, his back facing us. He owns That's A Wrap, a specialty gift wrap and stationery store in town, so he comes home in spurts when he's got coverage at the store. Mom's on the phone, probably checking in on the nurse staffing at Holly General before her shift tonight. But Mariah Carey is on the playlist, the fire's roaring behind the screen, and the midafternoon sun has set just below the trees.

It's holiday perfection.

"Tinola's ready!" Dad turns, carrying a tray of small bowls. The soothing smell of ginger wafts in the air, and the announcement of his specialty, a chicken soup with green papaya that six out of six of us love—or seven, if you count Carm—makes my mouth water.

"My stomach hurts," Irene whines, lying prone on the carpeted floor in front of the fireplace.

"Mmm-hmm." I eye her. "Told you that cup of hot chocolate would do that."

She sticks her tongue out at me.

"I'll keep trimming the tree." Carm hangs another ornament. "Besides, if I eat here and show up at home full, Trish'll be irritated."

Carm calls her parents by their first names: Trish and Frank. Mom laughs, but if I did that . . . well, I don't even try.

"I'll help you decorate," Dad decides as I grab the tray of soup from him. Dad's biggest thing is keeping everyone happy, occupied, and entertained. He eyes the watch on his wrist. "I've got another half hour before I have to head into work."

I pass out the bowls to Mom and the twins at the kitchen table. With only half of us seated, it's a relief to stretch out, though at the same time it's like I'm missing half my limbs.

As Dad cajoles Irene and Carm into singing one more Christmas song, I sip my soup from a large spoon and revel in the comfort in my belly. Around the table, Mom's, Grant's, and Graham's faces are turned down into their bowls. The routine is so ingrained that a pang shoots through me. In a few months, I'll be the one missing from this table.

And yet, what accompanies this thought is a frisson of excitement. Because it means I'll be wherever I need to be. Studying in Syracuse's grand library. Walking through campus with new friends. Settling into a chair in a lecture hall.

"Why didn't we mark these branches?" Dad growls from behind us, fluffing through the branches of the tree. "They're uneven."

I look up from my bowl to the others at the table and meet Mom's eyes, which crinkle in a smile. Dad is as predictable as the Grinch is grumpy. His next question will be about tinsel.

"Why do we keep buying tinsel when it gets everywhere?" he huffs.

And then, of course, the lights.

"Ay nako, these lights! We need to buy another box. Maybe two."

A giggle rises up from inside me—I can't help it. Dad always does this, while Mom hangs back, makes a cup of coffee, and allows him to do his thing until he relinquishes control. Then

Mom will wrangle the rest of the decorations with great stylistic precision. Everything will go up smoothly in the end, and it will be beautiful.

Reliable, just the way I like it.

My phone rings in my pocket—it's the theme song from *Holiday by the Lake,* which means it's Ms. Velasco. Mom flashes me a look—a meal at the table means no phones. Even if it is from her best friend and my boss.

"Please?" I stick out my bottom lip. "Maybe it's about more hours."

She presses her lips together, but after a beat of silence, she nods.

Yes. Pressing the green button, I stand and head toward the hallway. "Hello?"

"Lila, dear. How are you?" Ms. Velasco's voice is like a mouse's with its toe pinched in a trap.

"Fine." I frown. "Is everything okay?"

"Overall, yes. Specifically? No. We have a leak at the Inn, and we're short-staffed. I need to stay on the Inn-side because I have the plumbers coming. Can you come in and relieve me at the gift shop? I know it's last minute."

I open my mouth to accept, but then I turn back to the scene in the living room. With Dad leaving for work soon, and Irene perpetually not in the mood, Mom will need my help to put all of these boxes away before her 11:00 p.m. shift. Cleanup is the other half of this yearly event. I bite my lip.

Mom hovers at the end of the hallway, a steaming refill of soup in hand. "What is it, Iha?"

"Ms. Velasco needs help at the gift shop. The Inn has a leak."

"Tell her you'll go, so long as you're back by ten."

"Really? Thank you!" With that, I confirm my arrival with Ms. Velasco, and after letting Carm know, I head to my room to change into my uniform.

Minutes later, as I step outside the front door, Mom holds me back. "Lila?"

"Yeah?"

She gives me a meaningful look. "Remember that with struggle, there's opportunity."

It's the same thing she told Dad when he almost lost his business four years ago. It's meant to be motivational, but I also remember that, for Dad, things got worse before they got better.

And worse is not on my to-do list.

Chapter 3

My mother's advice echoes through my head as I leave my neighborhood and enter downtown, passing a wood and stone marker that says HOLLY, NY. HOME OF HOLIDAY BY THE LAKE.

Holly has a population of 14,533, a statistic I've memorized because it's part of my job. (Tourists are very interested in these little pieces of trivia.) It's also on the map as one of the most festive places to be during the holidays, which is immediately evident from the town's decorations. Holly doesn't play with measly decor. Each light post is wrapped in a netlike array of colored lights and has a snowflake fixture hanging from it. LED lights outline awnings and window frames that blink in coordination with the music being piped through downtown. From afar, the trolley rings its bells, and carolers positioned at opposite ends of the town sing holiday tunes. The town square's Christmas tree, a fifty-two-and-a-half-foot majestic spruce, is lit by twenty-five thousand bulbs and sports a star that's about five feet across. (More trivia!)

And it's not just for Christmas and New Year's. Holly's holiday decor is up half the year, only to be replaced by Valentine's Day, Easter, Independence Day, and fall themes.

But it doesn't mean that the joy is always year-round. Four winters ago, a bad snowstorm caused a massive branch from an ancient oak tree to fall onto Dad's store, collapsing the roof. We scraped by because of Mom's job, but our family struggled in the subsequent years.

The struggle was facing Christmas with no presents. It was watching my parents field phone calls from banks and insurance companies. It was seeing gossip spread like wildfire in town. After Ms. Velasco set up a HelpFund that exceeded its initial goal, people speculated that the accident could have been avoidable. Dad should've trimmed his trees like a good citizen, they said. Why should he benefit from all that free money? Maybe he even did it on purpose.

Even worse than the gossip? The fact that my family was doxed. Someone posted our home phone and address in one of the local community boards. It was taken down, but not before a person, or people, took note. We lost our privacy. Mom and Dad were constantly receiving nasty snail mail. We had to disconnect our landline.

Once, after getting dropped off late from Carm's house, I came across someone lurking near our house, though they ran off when Mrs. Ferreira parked. She called the police from inside her locked car—it wasn't the first time the police would be at our home. But no one could say for sure who it was and why they were there. Though it didn't matter, because the damage was done. I remember feeling afraid for a long time. My parents hovered protectively over us and were ultra-cautious of their surroundings; they forbade us from participating in social media. To this day, my parents are jumpy about anything to do with sharing personal information.

The bright side—or, as Mom might say, the opportunity? Dad spent more time with our family while he slowly rebuilt That's A Wrap. I got to know Dad better than I ever had. I learned the value of a dollar. And I made the decision that I don't want to burden my family more than I have to, with college and beyond. They'd saved some college money for me, but I decided I would make up what I could with scholarships, loans, and jobs. That, when I graduated from college, I would make enough money to support myself and help my siblings. That I would find work aligned with a reliable, well-paying profession. Which meant pre-med, and eventually becoming a doctor.

But something else came from that fear: this need to express myself. I had just started the free library, and I was reading more than ever with all the ups and downs. Books distracted me; they gave me hope. I felt so strongly about certain books that I would journal about them in my spiral notebooks. Winter break of my sophomore year, after getting hired at the Bookworm Inn, Ms. Velasco shared some *Holiday by the Lake*–inspired blog posts from megafans, and the idea was born. I could pay forward the hope books had given me. I could blog from my laptop, even from my phone, anonymously, and for free. I could do it before or after my shifts.

Blogging was against my parents' rules. But it made me happy, and for those moments, struggle was nonexistent. And it wasn't social media, technically. I wasn't sharing any of my personal information.

A mile east of downtown Holly, I flip on my turn signal and pull onto Bookworm Drive. The road leads into a dark canopy of tree branches that blocks out the moon, and the Bookworm

Inn appears along the horizon like a beacon of light. The Velascos took over the Inn—which used to be an estate owned by one of Holly's first residents—decades ago and restored it to its previous splendor. The town had gone through its own rough period when the local paper mill shut down, and the Inn was one of the reasons why the town survived—it employed many of its residents. But it was Ms. Velasco who brought in tourists from all over the country and expanded the business in a major way.

I park behind the gift shop just as the back door slams open. Ms. Velasco stomps out in her galoshes and slicker, her face scrunched in a serious expression. That is, until her eyes lock on mine.

Her face relaxes. "Oh, Lila. Thank you. I . . . There's so much going on. We've got a store-full."

"No problem." I lift up a plastic bag, which holds a takeout container full of warm tinola. "From my mom."

"Ah, she's St. Nick in human form. If you can put it in the refrigerator in the break room, it will be my reward for making it through all of this."

"What would you like for me to do?"

"I've got a plumber and everyone who has any expertise in water damage at the Inn, trying to fix the leak." She hikes up her hood. "I need to deal with one of the guest cabins. Apparently it has a malfunctioning window. That pretty much leaves Teddy on his own in the gift shop."

"Teddy's still here?"

"He was supposed to head back to school tonight, but he was kind enough to stay until I got help."

"Does he know what he's doing?" I flush, hoping my question doesn't sound too rude, but Ms. V doesn't seem to notice.

"He got the four-one-one on stocking the floor, and he knows the basics of the register—he's worked retail before—but . . . you'll see. Anyway, I'm not sure how long it's going to take, and you're the only one who answered their phone. I left messages, so I can only hope we get more backup." She winces. "I'm sorry."

"It's totally fine. I'm glad I can help. I want the hours."

"Great!" Her face lights up for a beat. "And just between you and me, there's something exciting coming down the pipeline. I can't breathe a word about it yet, not until next weekend's staff meeting, but it's changing the game."

"Oh, really?" Ms. Velasco's words pique my curiosity. Changing the game? How much busier and more successful could the Inn get? The gift shop barely has a lull during the holidays, and the Inn's reservations are solid through the middle of January.

"Yep. Here, grab the keys to the register." They're hanging precariously on her pinky, and I snatch them before they fall.

She walks backward, clearly in a rush. "I'll be back as soon as possible."

"Okay!" I wave and enter the back door.

The dull roar of customers fills the hallway, and I speed up.

Wow, it's busy.

In the throng of people, I spot Teddy's dark hair. He's at the register, ringing up a customer, with a line five deep.

"I'm sorry, sir." His voice rises above the rest. "I can't seem—"

"Look, can you get someone else to help you?" The customer's voice emits the truest sound of discontent.

My customer service smile goes on at full wattage, and I slip behind Teddy.

"Oh my God. Thank you," he breathes out. "I can't seem to—"

"He can't open the register," the customer—a man wearing a

32

Niagara Falls cap with a matching shirt—states, red-faced. "All I want is my change. Forty-nine cents."

"I mean. The thing won't open." Teddy frowns and presses random buttons.

"Whoa-kay," I say. "Hold up."

Teddy and I switch spots. I palm a button on the side of the register, and the drawer pops open with a satisfying ring. I scoop up forty-nine cents and drop it into the customer's hand.

The man levels Teddy with an exasperated expression. "Really?"

"It's tricky," I say with a shrug, even though it's not. "Thank you for your patience, and I hope you come back soon."

The customer leaves with a huff.

"Geez," Teddy mumbles.

Our introduction yesterday was casual and brief. Closer now, and less than a foot away, I get a better look at Teddy—at the one curl of hair that swoops just above his right eye, at the mole that's perched on his right cheekbone. At how the Bookworm Inn polo shows the outline of his muscled shoulders.

Muscles.

But instead of attraction, or even empathy at his current predicament, annoyance courses through me. If I had simply been given these hours instead of Teddy, the gift shop would not be this chaotic.

Since there's no time to teach Teddy how to work the register, because the next customer is waiting for their turn, I say, "Listen. Why don't you head out to the floor and clean things up or answer questions while I do this?"

"But I want to learn what you're doing here."

Annoyance escalates to irritation. "This is not the time for it, frankly." As if to prove my point, the bobblehead display of Max, the stray corgi in the film and the real hero who leads present-day Estelle to Leo for their second meet-cute, crashes to the ground. The resulting gasp from customers and the sound of a toddler crying cause me to inhale deeply. "Now will you go?"

"Fine." He leaves my side.

My focus shifts and I motion for the next customer. The line consumes me as I cashier and bag and greet, and I manage to all but forget about Teddy.

After the rush is over, a mere half hour later (though it felt like two hours at least), I clean up behind the counter and then return loose items back to their correct locations in the store. Yet, upon quick inspection of the floor, the bobblehead display isn't stacked where it's supposed to be. The throw blanket display is empty, and the earrings are nestled in the tea and coffee section.

Gritting my teeth, I round the corner and come upon Teddy. He's chatting with a customer in the free library, a couple of books under his arm, like time is as plentiful as snowflakes.

How long has he been standing here?

And in my area?

Okay, so the free library isn't *my* area, technically—I'm not paying rent—but I am in charge of it. And the unstated rule is that I'm the one who reshelves and stocks the books.

An unknown force draws me to Teddy and this customer, though neither look up at my approach. On the way, I pick up discarded items on the floor and almost trip on a stuffed animal of Dot, Estelle Mendoza's cat and the film's prankster.

By the time I reach their side, the heat of my impatience has shown itself through beads of sweat at the nape of my neck.

"Teddy." My voice is sharp, and I glance quickly at the customer, trying to keep my professional face in place. "Hello there."

"What's up?" Teddy's voice is all relaxation and ease.

"Can I speak to you for a moment?"

"Uh, okay. It's great to meet you." He nods at the woman, who has brown hair and skin, with a bandana tied like a headband around her head. She doesn't look familiar to me, but my delight at a new library visitor is dampened by my frustration at Teddy's inability to follow directions.

"Great to meet you. Can't wait to see what you send."

Send what? I frown. "Do you see what I have in my arms?" I ask him once the woman walks away.

"Yes. Looks like a bunch of touristy junk."

I level him with a glare. "Not junk—product. You were supposed to be keeping the floor maintained. Part of the job is picking up and putting things where they belong." I push the items into his arms.

"I was talking to a customer," he says belligerently.

"Library customers aren't paying customers. Gift shop customers are. And gift shop customers appreciate pretty displays." I gesture to the sad pile of corgi bobbleheads, which Teddy moved into a different corner.

"Those were in a precarious place anyway. If I build it back up, someone else is bound to run into it."

I open my mouth to rebut, then shut it again. He's right—I actually said the same thing to Ms. Velasco when the shipment came in last week. But that isn't the point. "Just please, set it up like it was before."

He shrugs. "Fine."

"Great," I grumble, and move past him to the books in the library that are clearly out of place from the day's rush of customers. I smile at this auspicious sign—people have been in my library! So I reshuffle them into their proper spots, wiping away the last bit of dust on the shelves.

A bright purple cover catches my attention as I straighten the books on the freestanding table, a catchall for discarded books or new donations. I fish it out—it's unfamiliar, titled *The Book of Holiday Surprises*. The cover shows a girl holding books close to her chest, surrounded by a weird glow, with lockers behind her that are decorated with wrapping paper.

It was published five years ago, and yet it's the first I'm hearing of it. I scan the first paragraph, consuming words like the Inn's snowplow after a storm.

In the background—in my real life—I hear the faint jingle bells of the back door, but I mentally bat away the distraction.

A shadow darkens the page, and I raise my head. It's Ms. Velasco.

The sounds of the gift shop rush back, and suddenly it's so bright. "Oh, hi." I straighten, embarrassment and heat rushing through me, an explanation at the tip of my tongue. I feel like my twin brothers after I find wrappers of chocolate-covered marshmallows on their bed. "Um . . . I was just putting things away."

"Oh, what? Of course." Ms. Velasco's expression is harried. Her gaze darts around the room, as if taking in the status of the gift shop in one swoop. "Lila, thank you for stepping in here like you did."

"Yeah, of course."

"You did a great job training Teddy. It looks like he's getting the hang of it."

Behind her, Teddy is building the bobblehead display on the windowsill—*not* where it's supposed to be.

I press my lips together to keep the objection from flowing

from my lips. *This* is Teddy learning? It's more like him objecting and resisting. "Thank you . . . yeah . . . though I'm not sure he did the same kind of retail? He could use a few more days of training."

"You're right. And this is our busiest season, which means that we need our best on the floor."

"Exactly." I nod.

"Like you."

My words fly out before I can stop them. "Yes, like me! Any shift. Any day."

This is my in. And Teddy is out.

A grin blossoms on her face. "I'm glad you agree, because while I was in the middle of the plumbing emergency, I was thinking . . . since you were looking for more hours, how do you feel about training Teddy? You'd simply jump into three of his shifts and guide him through my checklists. He starts next weekend, in fact—just in time for your winter break. That would free me up for other duties, which I desperately need to tend to."

I open my mouth to answer, but nothing comes out. While the hours would be great, it's not worth the headache if all Teddy does is fight me.

Ms. Velasco seems to clock my hesitation. "Just . . . think about it, okay? You can let me know at our staff meeting next week. I think it's a good fit. You're a natural leader."

"I'll . . ." My voice croaks, so I try again. "I'll think about it."

The last of the customers in the gift shop shuffle toward the register, the sound capturing our attention. At fifteen minutes to nine, closing time, only a handful are left in the shop.

"Why don't I take registers with Teddy and you take the floor," Ms. Velasco says quickly. "Start the cleanup for closing?"

I nod, eager for space. Starting from one end of the store,

which is the worse for wear, I fold T-shirts and set them back on tabletops, clean display cases, and return products to their rightful places. At the register, Ms. Velasco assists Teddy. For her, he smiles and feigns interest. He nods without a question when she corrects him.

So it's just to me that he's such a jerk.

I end my shift in the library area. As I clock out, Ms. Velasco hands me the book with the purple cover with a pensive smile.

It's a small extra reward for the night with Teddy, but I'll take it.

Chapter 4

My sister, Irene, is starfished on my bed, my comforter bunched around her, when I arrive home. She's got one of my graphic novels held above her, so engrossed that she doesn't notice when I pad inside.

Not until I swipe it from up top.

"Hey!"

"Hey yourself." I raise an eyebrow, which gets her moving.

She scrambles to sit up and crosses her legs under her. She has a sheepish look on her face, so I toss back the graphic novel. Enabler, I am.

"I'll remake your bed, promise." Under her breath, she adds, "Even if it makes no sense, since you're going to sleep soon."

I toss my keys onto my desk; I notice that my laptop, though closed, is not where I left it earlier today. "Irene. You know my rule . . ."

"Yeah, yeah. Don't mess with your things."

I spin and lean on the desk. "Like my laptop."

"I was just looking stuff up."

"Does Mom know?" I narrow my eyes. My parents are still

sticklers for internet rules: school research only, no social media, and supervision while watching YouTube. In Mom's words, *I trust you, but not the Internet.* And she means it with a capital *I,* as if it were a specific being. Though years have passed since the tree branch incident, the HelpFund, and the harassment, they are far from forgetting it, even if the rest of the world has moved on.

As the *ate,* I'm beholden to remind Irene of these rules. Mom's fears aren't superficial—I, of all my siblings, remember what they went through the most.

Even if I carry the simmering guilt that I've been breaking their rules for a couple of years now.

"Yes," she hisses. "I have a project for school due."

"All right. But next time, ask me." I gesture at my sister's phone, facedown on my bed. "There is such a thing as texting."

"I get it already," she huffs, cheeks blown out so they're taut.

It takes all of me to stifle my laughter. Even if I tried, I can't stay angry for long, not at her. Sisterhood is a constant push and pull. Truth is, despite our outward differences—that her hair is markedly curly and mine is straight, that she will be far taller than me once she's through puberty, and that no, she never makes her bed—on the inside we're so much alike.

We planners; we're both curious. She loves books—and book people are really the best people.

"What were you looking up?" I relent, sitting on my chair.

"Paint colors."

Inside, I beam at my inadvertent catch. "Sooo . . . not for a school project."

"I mean." Her cheeks turn a darker shade and her eyes dart all around me like she's tracking fireflies. She starts to mumble. "Well, first what I did was—"

Her reaction is enough of a lesson, so I take her out of her misery. "For paper or walls?"

"Ha . . ." She breathes out, chest caving in with relief. (Note to self: Tell Carm about this later.) "Walls. For when you leave."

"Geez." I cross my arms. Okay, so maybe I should have let her suffer more. "You're already calling it your room when I haven't even left."

"You have the room with the biggest closet. It's not personal."

I snort out a laugh. "It's not?"

"Nope. It's all about space planning." She throws her arms out wide. "Mommy told me that this is a ten-by-ten room. That's one hundred square feet I get to do anything I want with."

She explains her plans, and my gaze migrates around the room to all of my personal touches. The pictures taped up above my bedside dresser. The tapestry hanging on the wall behind my bed, because Dad is convinced anything heavier than that is bad luck. The rosary Mom tacked up above my light switch. My room isn't a Wayfair catalog. My stuff doesn't match; my decor is a mesh of my various interests. But it's full of things I love.

My tummy drops at the thought that this room won't be mine for much longer, though I try to push it away. It's silly, because I'll be going someplace new and exciting, a blank space, with so much opportunity. But there's this niggle of something I can't explain. That all of this effort, this sense of ownership, can be erased with a coat of paint.

Suddenly I see Teddy in my mind and think of his abrupt invasion in my life. No, he isn't like Irene, who's been waiting for her turn the last few years. Teddy doesn't seem happy to be here. He should feel lucky that he found a job in Holly's number one tourist destination.

41

Irritation rises up inside me, and I wait until Irene pauses in her description of her plans for the room. "Whew. These are great ideas. But I'm ready for some shut-eye," I say.

"I wasn't even done with my sentence." Her eyes narrow, and she slides off my bed. "Something's up with you."

"Do you mean besides having a little sister that can't take a hint?" I spin her by the shoulders, shuffle her out of my bedroom despite her objections, and close the door.

The silence that descends is both a relief and a bummer.

Only one thing can take me out of this funk. I pull out *The Book of Holiday Surprises* from my backpack, settle myself onto my bed, and turn to the second page, where I left off at the gift shop.

My unease dissipates as I dive into the story. Teddy, college fund money, Irene redecorating—all of it fades. My body relaxes; I breathe easier. I let the story scoop me into a magical sleigh and take me away, into the book's setting.

Three hours later, at almost two in the morning, in a jumble of emotions, I finish. I tuck myself into my bed and look up at the ceiling, at the singular dot of a remnant glow-in-the-dark star I put up my freshman year. My vision blurs; my eyes shut.

But sometimes, with a book that takes me in so quickly and doesn't let go, I'm left with a feeling of emptiness. It's like a low-level mourning that I've lost the experience of reading the book for the first time.

This is a book hangover.

I switch positions in bed, flip the pillow to the cool side, push the covers down to my feet, and then pull them all the way up toward my head. I look up at the ceiling once more.

It's a sign.

I have to write about this book.

But *The Book of Holiday Surprises* is still nagging at me, not only because I know I have to post about it, but because of its title.

Holiday surprises.

I sit up in bed with a lightbulb moment.

Surprises. For my readers. I can do a giveaway of my most favorite books to start. And I'm going to write up lists of books of certain tropes. Like *Top Ten Books About the Chosen One,* or similar.

That's how I'm going to step up the content this year.

I try to discern the sounds around me. Our house is cozy; the walls are thin, and Dad's snoring stands out over the low roar of the furnace. Tiptoeing to my door, I peek out for signs of Irene's sleep-walking, but it's pitch-black except for the blinking tree lights that create starlike projections on the wall and reflect the ornament boxes that were pushed aside to be put away tomorrow. Mom is at work until morning.

All clear.

A grin makes its way to my lips. I plop into my desk chair and flip my laptop screen up. When it wakes, Ariana Grande's trilling voice amplifies through the speakers—my sister's playlist—and I all but pound on my keyboard to quiet it. My heart races. *This* is why I do most of my blog posts at the Inn; in this house, my privacy is never guaranteed.

I take a deep breath, turn down the screen's glow, then head to my blog dashboard and type in my credentials.

The glimmering Tinsel and Tropes's blog header, illustrated by Carm, greets me. I click on the New Post button.

TINSEL AND TROPES
A HOLIDAY BOOK BLOG

Title: The Book of Holiday Surprises by T.A. Jones
CATEGORY/GENRE: YA CONTEMPORARY WITH
PARANORMAL ELEMENTS

*NOTE: read on after this post for a special
announcement from Tinsel and Tropes*

When is the right time to say no?

I found *The Book of Holiday Surprises* in a pile
of donated books, and it gripped me from the first
page. You all know that I tend to judge and read
books from the first paragraph rather than the back
cover copy, and at a time when I wanted to get the
heck out of reality, this book gave an escape.

Yes, it's been that kind of a week.

But back to the book and our protagonist.

Magic seems like a gift at a time when our
protagonist needs it most. She just moved to a new
school before the holidays (now *that* is a lump of
coal!), and her fellow classmates are predictably
unwelcoming.

Later on, we find out that her classmates
aren't who they portray themselves to be. That's
right—this won't be a spoiler if you read the back
copy—it is, in fact, a school filled with kids who
have supernatural abilities, and in her discovery of

her own powers through a book she finds in the locker she's been assigned, she uncovers their plot to overthrow the human world. And let's just say, that while the school breaks for the holidays, the characters in this story are far from lazing around eating cookies.

Told you it was good.

On top of that, we've got the villain's brother, who rejects magic out of principle and therefore is hesitant of our protagonist. She's wary of *him* because of his lineage and . . .

Yes, dear readers, my favorite trope: slow burn, and, on that note, opposites attract (read it and you will agree), in addition to The Chosen One.

It works out in the end. That's not a spoiler! The back cover already spills this. But there's a lot of drama in this book's journey, and heartache too. The story is well written, the plotting is tight, but it does make me question if our protagonist should have chosen magic. Would it have been better for her to have lived a simple life? To have averted her attention, to look elsewhere for answers or fulfillment?

Then again, she wouldn't have met a certain someone, and she wouldn't have discovered how powerful she truly is.

So, does that make all the pain worth it?

Choices are never easy to make; there usually seems to be an easy, safe route and a riskier choice.

One that involves stretching yourself. Probably reaching for areas unknown. The payoff? It could be great. But it's not without its bumps and bruises.

What would you choose?

Pros: While this is a romance, there is so much friendship in this book too. And self-discovery, which hit the spot for me.

Cons: Could have been a little longer. I really liked the villain in this story. TBH, I hope that the next story is the villain's!

Recommended for: Anyone looking for an escape. Once you start . . . just clear your calendar!

Rating: 4.75 stars

***

Note from Tinsel and Tropes: Thank you for reading to the end of this post! A heads-up that our blog's second anniversary is on January 2. Expect a special surprise!

Chapter 5

"*Someone's* moving slow this morning."

I recognize my coworker's voice without looking, and as I fill my Styrofoam cup with coffee, I quip back, "*Someone* is almost late."

KC cuts in line behind me to no one's objection and fills up a cup for himself. I barely finish stirring in a pound of creamer before he pulls me by the sleeve to the first row of chairs, set up in front of the cash registers. It's reliably free among the fifty chairs to accommodate the employees of the Bookworm Inn, because no one wants to be up close and personal during a staff meeting.

I plop onto the seat, the chill of the plastic chair doing nothing for my exhaustion. It's been a long week, starting with waking up late on Monday morning after writing and editing my blog post, which snowballed into the drudgery of reviewing for finals and work.

At the thought of my last blog post, my insides tingle. It garnered the most comments I ever had; readers were stoked to congratulate me in advance for the blog's anniversary, and wrote that they were excited for the upcoming surprise. Many also weighed in on the post's final question about choices. A clear majority wrote that they would have chosen magic versus the safe choice.

Me? If pressed, I might have sided with taking risk, but internally, I'm still undecided. Risk is real. It's scary, uncomfortable, and has consequences.

"Anyway, I'm not late. The range of arrival is between oh-seven hundred to seven-ten, and it is seven-ten." With a free hand, KC brushes back his hair, the tips glistening with melted snow. "To be honest, I had to go forty through downtown. My car had a hard time cranking up this morning and I thought I was going to be late. I'm just glad I didn't get pulled over."

The speed limit through Main is twenty miles an hour. I raise my eyebrows. "KC."

"I know, I know. I feel guilty thinking about it." He sighs.

"You're lucky Chief Dasher or any of his reindeer didn't get you."

"For real." He snorts. "Reindeer. That's cruel."

"I can't help it." Chief Dasher is, in fact, the chief of police's name, but the coincidence is hard to ignore. "This is Holly, after all."

"Then why do you look like you're an extra on *The Walking Dead*?"

"Gee, thanks. Always keeping it real."

"You know what I'm saying."

I shiver, and as if reading my mind, the shop's furnace clicks on. The temperature dropped a good ten degrees since yesterday, a true sign that winter is here. "Studying for finals. Three baby-sitting shifts, with parents sneaking out to buy Christmas presents. And it's sugar rush season for the kids." I shake my head to free myself of the memory of last night's gig. "Do you know that Magic Eraser actually erases crayons off walls? Takes a lot of elbow grease and a couple layers of paint, but still. It works."

"Blergh." He sips his coffee. "So update me. What's up with your full-time hours? I didn't get mine. Something about a new employee."

"I didn't get mine either, and yes. It's her nephew." I catch KC up on Ms. Velasco's offer to train Teddy.

"Is he even here?"

I glance around. "Doesn't look like it. He's supposed to start this weekend, though. And I'm supposed to give Ms. Velasco my answer today." I tip the cup to my lips, and the smell of java hits my nose, waking me up. Undoubtedly, the scent is the best part of coffee, because I'm not a fan of anything bitter.

"What are you going to say?"

I shrug. "Honestly? I don't know."

The chatter quiets as Teddy walks through the door. He's bundled up, but he looks like someone who didn't get any sleep either.

KC glances back. "That him?"

"Yep."

"I mean, he *is* the owner's nephew. Should you say no to training him?"

I press my lips together so as not to let my less-than-complimentary opinions gush out, but KC's words settle into me. Teddy and I had one shift together, and looking back, the night was busy and chaotic. Did I give him enough of a chance? Maybe I was making a choice based on a flawed impression.

"Well, he's cute." KC shrugs out of his coat. "He's got that tired, cuddly look about him."

"He's all yours."

"Nope." KC grins. "I'm taken."

KC is on cloud nine with his long-distance boyfriend, Seb, who is away for his first year of college. They're probably the sweetest couple I know. "Anyway, it isn't me who needs to have some fun," he says.

"What is it with you and Carm trying to add to my schedule? Last night, she sent me a shared calendar of our activities during break." I show him my lock screen, riddled with calendar invites, and tell him about Mission: Holly. A blog notification pops up and I flip the screen down quickly.

"Oh, wow," KC remarks, eyebrows lifting. "That's serious business."

Carm, KC, and I are in the same bubble of friends at our high school, but we don't usually all hang out together. An idea lights up like Rudolph's nose. When KC's attention drifts, I send Carm a text.

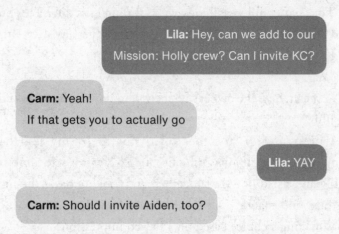

Lila: Hey, can we add to our Mission: Holly crew? Can I invite KC?

Carm: Yeah!
If that gets you to actually go

Lila: YAY

Carm: Should I invite Aiden, too?

Aiden O'Conner is another senior at our high school, and Carm's longtime crush.

I tug KC's sweater and show him my phone screen. "Hey, do you know what I think?"

He bends down and reads. "Really? Are you sure I won't be crashing?"

"No way. The more the merrier, right?"

"Okay. I'm in."

Just then, Ms. Velasco strides in and makes her way to the front of the room. She looks fresh-faced and awake; in fact, she's buzzing with energy this morning.

KC and I raise our eyebrows at the same time.

"Something's up," he whispers.

"Agreed," I say, remembering Ms. Velasco's excitement the other night.

She pulls a stool from behind the register and perches upon it. The room quiets, and her red lips part into a smile. "It looks like everyone's here. Thank you for coming this morning. Today's staff meeting won't run like usual—as a matter of fact, we have a lot of planning to do." She pauses, her eyes brightening. "Because Jonah Johanson and Remy Castillo are coming here. Right here, to the Bookworm Inn!"

It takes a beat to piece the puzzle together. To cobble the images of Jonah Johanson and Remy Castillo as Leo and Estelle, kissing next to the soaring trees, with Max's paws on Jonah's calves, as if trying to catch his attention.

Then my jaw drops.

The room explodes with conversation and clapping. The names of the two lead actors in the *Holiday by the Lake* film scatter in the air like glitter. I press my hands against my mouth and turn to KC, who is on his feet.

"Okay, okay, settle down, everyone." Ms. Velasco gestures for everyone to sit, though she's now standing, hands on her hips. "I know. It's pretty amazing. I didn't want to give everyone false hope before it was confirmed, but since this year is the twenty-fifth anniversary of the film's release, I thought why not try to get to the actors themselves? This is the culmination of months of work. Our team hassled and hustled. And now I'm so proud to present New Year's Eve by the Lake."

The lights dim to the dull roar of surprise. The inn supervisors move in coordination: one turns on the gift shop televisions, another flips up a laptop. The film's theme song pipes through the surround-sound speakers.

The room erupts in applause once more. My skin prickles with goose bumps.

Never have I looked forward to a PowerPoint presentation more.

Instinctively, I turn to gauge other people's reactions, to see if they're feeling the surge of emotions, too, when I meet Teddy's intense gaze. It's searing, and not full of the rest of the employees' joy and surprise.

Ms. Velasco's voice draws my attention to the front, though I can't get Teddy's expression out of my mind. For someone who's part of the family, he should be thrilled for this great news.

"New Year's Eve is a mere thirteen days away," she says. "*Thirteen*. But it was either New Year's Eve or never—these actors are busy and booked well out in advance, and it was by pure luck that one of my contacts pulled through. To be honest, I'm not worried about marketing or advertising. With our reach, this place will be packed. But here's the deal—we need to be ready for it." She clicks through to the slideshow, which covers everything, from schedules to work expectations, to inventory, decor, the general schedule of events, and ticket sales. There's a slide explaining the lottery for employees who want to work the event, and twice as much staff will be scheduled the day of.

Ms. Velasco pauses to sip water from a bottle. "There's a lot to be done from now until then. Everything is wonderful, don't get me wrong. You all do a magnificent job each and every day. But with some media descending on us when the actors arrive, as well as a bigger crowd than we usually expect in December, we have to discuss the inevitable: preparation and exposure." She lifts a piece of paper. "A cheat sheet. On the Inn's mission and history, et cetera, just in case people ask. Some of you already have this memorized. Others, on the other hand . . ."

Snickering filters through the crowd. KC pretend-covers his face, and I laugh.

"Everyone chosen to work the event must also read the book or watch the film before New Year's. We want you up to speed around the mega-fans as well as the actors."

It dawns on me then. Oh my God, Oscar nominees will be walking through our front doors in just *thirteen days*.

I don't take a cheat sheet and pass the stack to the row behind me. "Remy Castillo," I whisper to KC. "I can't believe it. Do you know that she's Filipino American?"

KC laughs. "Yes, Lila. You've only told me about a hundred times."

"Well this is a hundred and one. And did you know that—"

"That the author insisted that Remy was cast because she was also Fil-Am." He laughs. "You're liable to pass out when you meet Remy."

"I'm going to be a mess."

And, just like that, my exhaustion is nowhere to be found.

After the staff meeting, Ms. Velasco surprises all of us with treats from Jolly Cupcakes, Holly's specialty cupcake shop. When the tray is passed to me, the peppermint red velvet is still up for grabs. It's to die for; it tastes like the holidays, like snow and candy canes and a roaring fire, all in one. As the flavors blend on my tongue, I imagine what it will be like to meet Remy Castillo.

The front double doors will fly open, snow swirling in her wake, her dark hair blowing backward. Her face will be flawless, and though she's as old as my mother—literally two months and three days older—Remy's going to be wearing those iconic high-heeled boots from the film she shot a year after *Holiday by the Lake* called *The Fire Among Us,* where she played a Latina dancer.

"Earth to Lila." A hand waves in front of my eyes. I blink, and KC comes into view.

"Sorry, what?"

He nods toward the side of the room before peeling off the bottom of his mocha strawberry cupcake. "Ms. Velasco's been sneaking glances your way."

"She is?" I look beyond the crowd milling in the library area. Teddy's standing next to her. Ms. Velasco waves me over. "Yep, she is."

"Do you know what you're going to say about the training?"

"Nope."

"You've got about fifteen steps before you figure it out."

I heave a breath and head over. Weaving my way through my coworkers, my heart speeds up. Work more hours and deal with Teddy? Or try to pick up some odd jobs elsewhere for less money and keep some of my dignity?

As I approach the group, Teddy meets my eyes. For a beat, I'm caught up in his stare and the way he seems to be taking me in.

My temperature spikes, and whether he's checking me out or sizing me up, my first inclination is to look away. But my firstborn persona arises from my bashfulness. I don't shy away from a dare.

When I make my way to the group, there's only one open place to stand, and that's next to Teddy.

No big deal, right? And yet, it feels like it is.

While everyone is chatting among themselves, the silence between me and Teddy builds. I should really make conversation. Teddy is new, and our crew is small but tight. He wasn't the one who insisted he take my hours; it was Ms. Velasco's decision.

"Neat, huh? Celebrities . . . here," I lob at Teddy. He has one hand in his pocket, while the other holds the rolled-up cheat sheet. His posture is a weird mix of nonchalance and tension. On his dark pants are traces of white powder, like he ran his fingers against the fabric.

What is all that?

"Neat," he says.

His smile is polite, but he's clearly unenthused. Then again, we didn't leave things on a good note the last time we worked together. So I let his attitude roll right off me, even if he is impossible to ignore. Because as KC noted, Teddy is cute, and there's a hint of cologne—or maybe it's just him—that has made my nose perk up.

I cram a piece of cupcake into my mouth.

Maybe no should be my answer.

But when Ms. Velasco sets her attention on us with her beaming smile, I remember that Jonah Johanson and Remy Castillo are coming.

I want to be a part of these big plans for the Inn. I want the money.

"Lila, have you thought about it?" she asks.

"Yes, I have." I turn to Teddy once more. "I'll be glad to help."

Chapter 6

"You want me to go through this list?" Teddy lifts the laminated sheet, tucked into a clipboard, to his face. "Turn on lights. Turn on register. Unlock door. Check the thermostat." His eyes shift upward to me and then back down. "And you want me to physically mark the boxes next to it. Won't I be able to tell if the door's locked when the customers can't get in?"

A headache creeps into my skull, and his name is Teddy Rivera. I touch my temple, noting the time above the front door. Only ten minutes are left before we open, and the parking lot is already half filled with vehicles. Sunday is our busiest day, when most tour buses schedule their stop.

"Those lists are for everyone to use, written up by Ms. Velasco. So it's not just for you. Mark the list when you get through with the tasks, please." I hold up the dry-erase marker.

And finally, after a protracted moment, Teddy takes the marker and checks the box with a sigh.

It's going to be a long day. Admittedly, because Teddy was here before I arrived, and dressed properly in his uniform, I thought that better workdays were ahead. Nope—our last workday was actually just a preview, because Teddy cannot be taught a single thing.

Still, I move on and attempt to lead with patience and kindness. Three training shifts with Teddy—that's it. "Normally we have two to three people working the gift shop, while Ms. Velasco or one of the other managers float through the whole property. When we do have three or more working the shop, we try to make everything easier and have a helper with every cashier." I point to the two registers. "So if you're on the register, I'll be right next to you, packing things so that, as soon as the customer pays, I can hand them their package and keep the line moving."

He cups his chin with his hand, his lips pursed. It's a model move that makes me look away. How does he do it? How can someone be so attractive yet so utterly aggravating??

"Wouldn't it be better if we just open up a second register?" He looks up at the ceiling, as if someone's feeding him info from above. "Serving two in five minutes is better than serving one in four minutes, right? If you do the math . . . then in twenty minutes we serve eight customers rather than five."

I shake my head, and a laugh bubbles out of me. Yeah, looks definitely don't make up for attitude.

"You're saying I'm wrong? I'm a whiz at math. Puzzles too."

"No. Your algebra is right, but you've been here a day. How did you even estimate that it takes five minutes versus four minutes per customer? And you don't know how much concentration it takes to pack up these items. Many of the things we sell are fragile. Besides, these are Ms. Velasco's procedures, and we've been doing it this same way for years."

"But if everyone said that, then there wouldn't be new inventions, trailblazers. Whistleblowers."

"We are part-time employees in a gift shop, Teddy. And it's time to open the doors." I grit my teeth and refocus our conversation to the shadows of customers outside the front doors. This is a no-win situation, since Ms. Velasco is his aunt. She's who he'll need to contend with ultimately, not me.

"Yes, ma'am." He salutes me with a sarcastic grin.

As he lumbers toward the front, I put my phone away. Above all, Ms. Velasco's pet peeve is using our phones while working. But before I stick it under the counter, where a wireless charger sits, a notification from my blog lights up the screen:

> **[Tinsel & Tropes] IloveReading:** Putting this book down on my TBR! And can't wait for your blog birthday surprise.

It's followed by a text from Carm:

> Ready for our first Mission tonight? Make an Ornament night with Mrs. Claus?

I groan. It's thirty-five dollars for a glass ball ornament and glitter. But I *did* promise.

> **Lila:** How could I forget?
> You set my calendar to alarm this morning!

> **Carm:** KC will be there too
> 7pm
> You better not go MIA

I groan again.

"What's up with you?" Teddy asks, suddenly in front of me.

I startle. Goodness. He's inches away. And he smells good, like fresh laundry and mint. Mentally, I clamp down my sense of smell. "Nothing."

"You ready for me to open?"

"I said I was ready."

He sticks out a hand. I stare at it.

"The key?"

"Right. The key." I slap the silver ring into his palm.

"Thanks." Grinning, he walks away.

Carm: *How's the first day with Teddy?*

A grunting sound pulls my attention. Teddy is hanging from the door frame, using just the tips of his fingers. He pulls himself up so his elbows bend to almost ninety degrees. Then he casually lets go and unlocks and flips on the automatic doors.

I look around to see if anyone else witnessed that feat of strength and ridiculousness. Who does that? And why??

> **Lila:** I might need sugar after our crafting

> **Carm:** Ooo, because he's so sweet?

> **Lila:** Because I need all energy to deal with him

More dots indicate that Carm is responding, but at the sound of the doors sliding open and the footsteps of customers entering, I stick my phone back under the counter.

One thing at a time.

Four hours later, and still on the register, my energy drags. My life force is drained from dealing with Teddy.

No, we can't wait until the end of the day to return all of the go-backs.

Yes, we must greet every customer that walks in.

Yes, even when they're browsing.

No, heading into town for lunch probably isn't a good idea because you won't get back in time.

Fine, you can have half my sandwich.

To Teddy's benefit, having three younger siblings has trained me in all the ways. I'm somewhat patient when Teddy suggests rearranging the stockroom, because he couldn't find the candy cane magnets. I practice self-control when he comments that the register area is too cluttered. And when he tells a toddler that it's all right to "test" the music boxes by winding them all up and letting them play simultaneously (we have eight different varieties), I dial into my restraint.

Teddy is lucky that my exterior exudes calm, even if my insides are on hyperdrive, like a disgruntled elf on Christmas Eve.

A phone alarm sounds through the store, grabbing the attention of customers nearby, and from the corner I hear, "Yessssss."

Please tell me that he hasn't had his phone on him this whole time, I think. *And tell me he didn't turn on his alarm to signal the end of his shift.*

Sure enough, Teddy appears at the registers, carrying a box of stuffed animals, a grin plastered on his face. It would be adorable if he wasn't so frustrating. "Quitting time."

"Technically, you can't leave the store until your replacement gets here." Although, relief courses through me because shift number one with Teddy is dunzo.

"Hi! I'm here!" Shana, another gift shop employee, enters in a rush. She pulls her locs over a Bookworm Inn visor.

"Sweet. I'm off to clock out." Teddy holds out the box of products. "Once I drop these off in the stockroom, of course."

"Sounds good to me," I mumble. Good riddance. Shana is a whiz in the gift shop, and with her at the register, perhaps I can get a couple of minutes in my library. The last of the tours have come through, and at least two bags of donated books were dropped off today.

Teddy weaves through the aisles, whistling, and as he passes the sunglasses display, his phone thumps out of his back pocket.

"You dropped your phone," I call out.

"Can you grab it for me?" he asks, readjusting his grip on the box.

"I can, but do I want to?" I whisper. Except seeing that phone on the ground as a couple of customers enter the shop makes me nervous. "I'll put it under the counter!" I yell.

"Whatever!"

Jeesh.

How does that happen? How does Ms. Velasco, who is very much like my mother, and therefore much like me, have a nephew who's so . . . whatever?

I bend down and pick up the phone; it's protected in a black Smashbox cover, like mine. There isn't a day without a spill or a drop or someone stealing my phone in the Santos family, and Smashboxes are the best on the market. Of all the colors, the black cover is always on sale.

I stick his phone under the counter with mine.

A group of ladies passes our large wall of windows, all wearing the same teal shirt, with *Holiday by the Lake's* most famous quote scrawled across it: ALL I HAVE IS MY WORD, AND LOVE. They have matching hair accessories, too: shiny pink bows tied on top of their heads.

But that's not what startles me. Many a girls' trip have come through these doors, the Inn a crucial part of their pilgrimage. It's the sheer amount of bodies. Five, six, eight, twelve . . .

"Big group!" Shana yells as she peers through the window. "A bus! Yikes. Two buses!"

Teddy grunts a complaint from the back, but moments later he appears, exasperation and complaint written on his face at my impending question.

"Stay?" I raise a hand before he can comment. "I know, and I'm sorry. These tour companies usually call before they arrive."

"I can't."

"Can't? Or won't? Look, you can't bail right now. You can text Ms. Velasco, but until she gets here, we're going to be outnumbered." I bite my cheek to keep the rest of my thoughts at bay, aware of the customers entering the shop.

Finally, he answers with a hint of an eye roll. "Fine. But I'm not greeting them."

"That's okay with me." I scramble to the door and face the avalanche of teal and giggles.

Turns out, the Inn is bombarded, too, leaving Shana, Teddy, and me to work the crowd until there are only five customers left in the store.

Teddy's impatience is on display throughout the deluge. He sighs so loudly that I hear him above the roar of the crowd. His fingers drum against the counter in between each customer, and when one older lady who bought the replica straw hat Estelle wore during the film counted out quarters for payment, Teddy all but started to melt into a whimpering puddle like Frosty on a warm, sunny day.

As soon as he dumps the quarters into the till, I approach the counter. "Just go."

"You sure?"

"Absofreakinglutely."

A grin splits his face, like he didn't just spend the last ten minutes sulking. "Later." He slips a hand under the counter and grabs his phone, then heads to the back. As he passes Shana and enters the doorway that leads to the hallway, he leaps to grab the door frame, his fingers on either side, and just hangs there. Then he lifts his knees up to his chest. Another pull-up.

Shana jumps back and flashes me a shocked expression. "What the—"

I shrug. I don't even know what to say.

Chapter 7

While my favorite place inside the Bookworm Inn is my library, my beloved outdoor spot is its east side covered patio area that overlooks Otisco Lake and the famous pier where Leo proposes to Estelle. Its location is away from the parking lot, out of view of customers, and far enough away from the cabins, which means it's quiet and serene. It's the perfect place to take my breaks, where it can be just me and the book I'm reading.

I plop down on the Adirondack chair, my jacket puffing up to cover my chin, and pull my next book out of my jacket pocket. It's the first book in the mass market Hanukkah Hijinks cozy mystery series, called *Menorah Mayhem,* which I found in the free library pile. There aren't enough non-Christmas holiday books in circulation, and anticipation rushes through me at the prospect of reading a Hanukkah tale. I dig into the first page, and then the second, the third, and more, and the rest of the day fizzles away.

My phone buzzes several times in my pocket. It tears me from the story—I'm at page twenty-three and, good thing, at a scene break.

But when I flip my phone over to check the text notifications,

I notice that the lock screen photo isn't of a pile of books but of mountains. A moment later, more texts fly in—I don't recognize the names.

Hugh: *V7, baby!*

Penn: *Yo the way you matched your hands is absolutely heinous*

Hugh: *Yeah man just piano match and crank with your left*

Will: *And yeah that drop knee is absolutely ridiculous*

Cece: *That route's spicy*

Penn: *That move is just heavy tension bro. You've got to core in and pray*

Some of the words on the screen are broken up from the cracks that mark the glass.

My screen's broken.

"No way, no way." I'm always so, so careful with my things. This phone has to last me until I leave for school. As I sit up, irritation races up my spine. How did I switch my photo, break the screen, *and* mistakenly end up in a random group chat?

As a snowflake lands on the screen, I wipe it away, smearing water onto the glass and . . . Oh my gosh . . . "Where's my screen protector? What the H. E. double candy canes is going on?"

The phone buzzes in my hand with an incoming call, and I fumble it in surprise, dropping it onto my lap. The number that appears on the screen is familiar, though there's no photo assigned to it.

"Wait." I read the number again, aloud. "Two one four, six eight five, one one one . . ."

It's my phone number. What?

My thumb presses the green button instinctively, and my hand brings it to my ear. "Hello?"

"You have my phone."

It's an alien from the other world. I've been dropped into a scene where aliens take over the phones of . . .

"Lila," the voice says. "It's Teddy."

"Teddy?" My brain recalibrates. I pull the phone from my ear. Reread the phone number. Slowly, the facts come together.

"Oh my God, I have your phone," I say. "This isn't a plot to take over the world."

"What?" He laughs.

"N-nothing. I mean, I was confused, seeing the notifications."

"You read my notifications?"

"I couldn't help it! And . . ." The truth dawns on me. "You're calling me from my phone."

"I thought it would be faster than going all the way back to the Inn. And oh my God, why do you have a password with all ones? I took a chance, and it worked."

"It's for my brothers, since I let them use my phone." And because I hate passwords. Note to self: create a tougher one. I shake my head at my thoughts, which are going down the wrong chimney. "Wait. I'm confused."

"I took your phone, Lila. Accidentally. And I can't bring it back right this second. Can we meet later on tonight? Around midnight?"

"Midnight?"

"Yeah, I'm—"

"I can't meet at midnight. I'll be asleep by then."

"I can't do earlier. How about tomorrow?"

"Tomorrow? That's too far away. And I've got school."

"I don't mind meeting you early."

"Why is this so complicated?" What does he have to do that's so important that we can't exchange our phones until tomorrow??

From his side of the world, someone yelps. The phone muffles, and Teddy mumbles something, sounding far away.

"Hello?" I call out. "I'm still here."

"Yeah, okay. Sorry. Meet me at the Scrooge's Shack for breakfast. How early can you get there?"

"I mean . . ." I raise my fingers to my forehead, thinking of my schedule. "Seven, I guess?"

"Seven, then. See you—"

Now, thinking of his notifications, mine must be flashing on my screen too. From Carm or KC or geez, Irene, and maybe even my TnT blog notifications. *No!* I heave a breath to calm myself. There are character limits to notifications, and my blog notifications look so much like email ones. And since it's been a few days since I posted, none might come in while he has my phone. "Just don't snoop through my phone, and please, please take care of it, okay?"

"Yep." He clicks off. Without a goodbye.

But that's not what catches my attention. It's all the texts that continue to flow through this group chat.

Will: *Where are you T?*

Cece: *He's probably at that new job. Can't believe you ditched us for Holly.*

Will: *Not sure how you're going to manage new job and the thing we're not supposed to talk about*

Penn: *T don't take the L*

Cece: *Stay focused. You worked too hard*

Will: *We also need updates on the nemesis*

Penn: *Don't piss her off you might need her*

My eyes glom on to that message.

Nemesis. Is this text about me?

And what's "the thing we're not supposed to talk about"?

Here's what I know for sure: Teddy has a secret, one that could potentially affect work. Something simmers inside of me, like anger and vindication. He took my hours at the Inn, and for what? So he could be doing whatever he's doing?

My face burns. This is wrong, me reading his notifications, but it's not my fault, is it? They're just showing up in front of me. At least I didn't hack into his phone, like Teddy did to mine.

Behind me, the door opens, followed by Ms. Velasco's throaty laugh. "Lila! I know you're on your break, but I've got a customer here who wants a tour of your library."

I slip the phone into my pocket and stand, feeling equally relieved and guilty at the interruption. "Um, sure! I'm happy to give a tour."

As I head back to the Inn and go into my memorized tour, showing a white-haired older woman all the hard work I've done building this library, all I can think of are Teddy's texts.

If I'm the nemesis, what problem does he have with me? And what is he hiding?

"If you need help or have any problems, simply raise your hand," says Mrs. Delaney, who's dressed in an impeccable Mrs. Claus outfit, complete with artificial white hair and rosy cheeks. We're at our ornament-making class, which is the first item on our

Mission: Holly bucket list that we've managed to attempt—mostly because I've been working at the Inn all the time, as Carm keeps reminding me. As Mrs. Delaney speaks, I try to take in her tips on how to decorate the inside of a clear glass Christmas ball above the chatter in the packed log cabin.

Yet, despite her sincere enthusiasm—her job as a kindergarten teacher at Holly Elementary is at full display—I'm still confused. Why did I pay so much money for a fifty-cent glass ball, with instructions that leave so much room for interpretation? How this ornament-making event ended up ranking six on the list of things to do in Holly, I have no idea.

I raise my hand. Next to me, Carm sighs, and KC bites his lip to keep a laugh from escaping, but I forge on.

"Yes, Lila?" asks Mrs. Delaney.

"If I dribble the acrylic paint inside, won't the colors just mix together and turn brown?"

"Not if you go slow, dear. And try dripping it against the inside of the actual glass."

"And won't the glitter just clump up?"

"If you sprinkle it around, like this"—she does this with a flourish to demonstrate, all in a soprano tone—"you'll do just fine."

I raise my hand for another question, but Mrs. Delaney turns ever so slightly and takes someone else's question.

"We know what you need, Lila," KC whispers, loud enough for the table to hear. "A checklist."

"Har-har. Just because you and Carm are so artistic and I'm not. I've never decorated inside an ornament, only the outside. I need directions to a destination."

"What I really want is the star glitter. Did you see that being passed around?" Carm glances at the table behind us, at a family wearing matching hoodies that say MEET ME AT HOLLY.

"We can't just take someone else's glitter," I say.

"Why not?" A grin escapes her lips. Then she stands and meanders between the small square tables. "Got it." Carm sits, plopping the bottle of star glitter on the table.

"I like how you work," KC says.

"Same," Carm says. "Why haven't we hung out before?"

"Because high school," KC says.

Our conversation quiets with that thought. We attended preschool to senior year together, but it's only in the last year of working at the Inn that I got to know KC. It's weird to think that, even in our tiny town, there are still people to know and things to do. Like create ornaments.

I settle into my chair, then squeeze paint into my Christmas ball. From the get-go, it's a mess. The paint glops to the bottom of the ball with a large splat. "Son of a snowman," I mutter.

The table erupts into giggles. Meanwhile, my friends treat their project like they're Santa's elves themselves, handcrafting every toy for every good girl and boy with artistic magic. Soon, we settle into banter and teasing (I overanalyze every step, KC has hogged all the silver paint, and Carm has "borrowed" two other tables' star glitter) as we craft, and everything is right in the world. The money I spent becomes a distant memory, because this moment is priceless.

"Thank you for reminding me about Mission: Holly," I say, holding up my ornament. "Even if my ball is fugly."

"It's not fugly. It's . . . ," KC starts. "Interesting," he says as Carm chimes in with, "Full of personality."

They crack up.

"Uh-huh." I roll my eyes. Though inside, I feel lighter than marshmallows in hot chocolate.

"Let's make it a twofer," Carm says. "Number five on the top ten list is apple cider doughnuts at Comet's Cider."

"Ooooh." KC rests a hand on his belly. "My tummy just growled. I'm in."

Which makes me regret what I have to say next. "I can't."

Carm frowns. "Are you working again?"

"No, but I've got homework. And I've got to meet Teddy for breakfast first thing tomorrow morning."

The table falls into silence. KC's jaw drops.

"Excuuuuse me?" Carm stretches the word. "This is all levels confusing. This is *Teddy*, right? As in the one who took your hours?"

I wince. "It's a whole thing. He asked me to meet at Scrooge's."

Her eyes widen. "So, wait. You're going to ditch us tonight so you can meet Teddy tomorrow at Scrooge's Shack, which is number three on our Mission: Holly list?"

A part of me wishes I hadn't mentioned it. "I've got no choice," I insist. "We accidentally switched phones."

KC's eyes brighten. "Mmm. You switched phones? And that's all this is?"

I eye both my friends. "I swear it's nothing!"

"Ooooh, you're freakin' out. That just confirms there's something going on," KC says. Carm nods emphatically. "I see those shifty eyes. Tell us everything."

Double-teamed, I give in. I catch them up on the phone switch, Teddy's quirks, and the texts that popped up in his notifications. About his secret, and me, his nemesis.

"I can't imagine you being anyone's nemesis," KC says as he cleans up his workspace. Across the room, Mrs. Delaney announces that she'll be passing around velvet boxes for the Christmas ornaments.

"You haven't seen her with her sister," Carm retorts. "So why aren't you switching phones tonight?"

"He says he's busy until midnight, and there's no way I'm meeting him then."

I can see Carm's next comment coming like December twenty-five on the calendar.

"We should go find him!" she exclaims.

"No. No way."

"Way," KC agrees. He all but shoves his phone to me. "Find your phone."

"I . . . No. It's no big deal."

"Here, let me." Carm gets on her phone. "I know her login and password."

"I gave that to you just in case." I try to snatch her phone away. We're making such a ruckus that Mrs. Delaney clears her throat. I revert to my Goody Two-Shoes self and back down.

"This is one of those 'just in case' moments. Don't worry. We're going to be stealthy. Don't you want to know what Teddy is up to?"

I sigh, but after a beat, nod. There's no point in lying. As if I could get homework done knowing my phone's with Teddy. And while I'm not great at making ornaments, I can definitely snoop.

Chapter 8

Twenty minutes after Carm successfully logs in to my Find My Phone app, I kill the engine of my car behind KC's, who is parked behind Carm. If we were trying to be stealthy, we failed miserably, with our three cars traveling in close caravan to Mistletoe Lane at the northeasternmost part of town and then parking inches from each other on a road that butts up against the open expanse of fields.

This is a bad, bad idea. So I sit in my car with my hands on the steering wheel and mull over potential escape plans. I could simply restart the car, make a U-turn, and speed out of there. Or maybe I could feign sickness?

I look out into the darkness, beyond the sparse wire fence, to the building beyond. There are several cars parked next to it.

Something niggles at the back of my brain, a spark of a story. Maybe Teddy's part of a secret organization building a nuclear reactor that's supposed to intercept the next meteor headed straight to earth à la *Armageddon*. Or maybe it's a secret lab creating mold spores that turn the population into zombies, like *The Girl with All the Gifts*.

Whatever it is, it has everything to do with those messages I read earlier today.

Not sure how you're going to manage a new job and the thing we're not supposed to talk about.

A sudden pounding on my window makes me yelp, and I look to the passenger side, where both Carm's and KC's faces are plastered against the glass. "Oh my God! Don't do that!"

They burst into laughter and gesture for me to exit.

I shake my head; they both nod.

"Dang it." I open my door and step out into the cold night. From the building, there's a faint sound of music. "What even is that place?"

"My map shows it as an open field," KC says.

"Let's go find out," Carm adds.

I don't get a chance to object. My friends march toward the building, huffing and puffing determinedly in the cold air. "I feel like this is an invasion of privacy."

"And yet, he has your phone. If you're reading his notifications, then he's doing the exact same thing, so it's a mutual privacy invasion. Besides, I want to see this Teddy." Carm's profile gleams with mischief.

"Oh, he's cute," KC adds.

"Even better."

Feet away from the entrance, my friends stop, and I run into their backs. "Ooomph," KC says as he trips forward.

Nope, not stealthy.

"You lead the way, Lila." Carm pushes me toward the closed metal door.

"What? This isn't even my idea!" I protest.

Just then, the door opens with a wild screech. I jump back, barely missing being hit.

"Whoa. Watch out!" a guy yells. He's wearing short shorts, a tank top, winter boots, and a long coat. Not quite the norm for winter in the Finger Lakes. He marches straight to his car, passing KC and Carm without acknowledging them.

The echoes of voices inside draw me closer; I pull the door open and a stuffy smell wafts out. When I hesitate, Carm and KC nudge me forward into the bright light of a barn.

My gaze rises higher and higher, and then all around the room, where it takes me one, two, three seconds to orient myself.

There are bodies everywhere. Half clothed, climbing walls, hanging from structures, strapped in by ropes, some contorted into weird positions. I stumble forward as my friends pile in, gasping and giggling.

I tear my eyes away, barely able to watch in case someone falls. As I turn, I see a vinyl sign that says CLIMB HOLLY.

A climbing gym. In Holly. When did this happen?

"Whoa," Carm says.

"This is rad," KC adds.

A woman in a yellow long-sleeve Climb Holly shirt saunters in our direction. Her face is familiar, though with all the noise and sights of the gym, my brain can't place her. "Hi there, welcome to Climb Holly." She gives me a little wave, then pauses. "Wait a minute. Aren't you from the Bookworm Inn? I was there the other day, in the free library."

After a beat of concerted focus, I remember. "You were talking to Teddy that day."

"That's me! Amaya Reddy, owner of Climb Holly." Her smile is bright and inquisitive. "How can I help you all?"

"We . . . I . . ." A flash of red grabs my attention and I look up to a wall, where a person is hanging on for dear life. "I didn't know that we had a climbing gym in Holly."

"Oh yeah! We haven't done much advertising, but we've been open for a couple of months now."

"You have a lot of customers." At the sound of a sharp snap, my head jerks to a person on the ground adjusting a rope tied to his waist.

"Glad to say that the hard-core folks found us. The fall and winter seasons bring in even those who prefer to climb outside."

"Ah." I swallow back my nerves, imagining these people climbing actual mountains without the large pads to soften their landing, just in case they . . .

The thought brings about the sour beginnings of nausea.

"Do you want to take a look around?"

"Not really," I whisper.

But she doesn't hear me, because both my friends chime in and say, "Yes, we'll take a look around."

Amaya excuses herself after pointing out the highlights of the gym; Carm slinks an arm through mine and pulls KC by the hand. "Let's go."

I should pull back, but I, too, am drawn forward, watching the climbers move up the walls without fear and effort.

Even if I prefer my feet on the ground.

When I turn the corner, oddly shaped boulders with marked footholds and handholds take up real estate on the ground. The people climbing here don't have harnesses or ropes. Though they're only about ten feet from the ground, a couple of the climbers are all but perpendicular and totally unsupported.

My attention is drawn to one person on a boulder. His dark

hair is held back by a red headband. He's wearing a tank top . . . and his *arms*. They're corded and sinewy as he navigates himself under a ridge and while holding on with his left hand, dips his fingers of his right hand into the chalk bag strapped around his waist. He rubs the chalk between his thumb and fingers in an effortless and delicate motion, in contrast to his legs and left arm, which are flexed and tense.

Muscles.

"That is . . . ," Carm starts.

"Wow. It definitely is . . . ," KC continues.

The person hefts himself to reach the next hold with his right hand, before he lets go and drops onto the padded floor. His shoulders gleam with sweat, and when he turns, it's punctuated by a wide smile.

A wide smile on a familiar face that usually looks grumpy in my presence.

"Teddy," I gasp. "It's Teddy!"

Everything begins to make sense: the white chalky powder on his pants, the carabiners. His lock screen photo. How he can't pass a doorway without hooking his fingers onto the frame.

Teddy Rivera, who is slowly turning in my direction.

Jumping Jack Frost!

He can't see me here. He'll know I tracked him down.

My body has a split second to move, and I drag my friends behind a group of climbers who happen to be passing by, then speed to the front entrance, where Amaya is watching us with a grin. She shoves a flyer into our hands when we pass her. "Fun, right? We have a free trial period."

"Thank you!" And in my most natural and unhurried way, I run out the door, Carm and KC behind me, heaving in laughter.

Chapter 9

Scrooge's Shack is a corner restaurant on South Main and Sleigh, and when I round the block just shy of 7:00 a.m., dragging from my late night of sleuthing, my insides spark like too many lights plugged into a socket.

Teddy is sitting at a window-side booth in full view, head bent down over an open book, with a finger on the page. My heart flutters; it catches me off guard. I read that a quarter of the American population hasn't read one book in the last year. And it's rare I see someone my age reading a book in public. This is . . . compelling.

Then he raises his eyes and lifts a hand in a wave when he spots me on the sidewalk. And I swear that his face lights up. Again—weird.

But despite my best efforts, I tingle in this heart-stopping way and wave back. Hopefully that means that he didn't see that spectacle of failed debauchery last night. I, on the other hand, cannot unsee Teddy's display of strength and ability.

A car whooshes by, and the sound of its wheels on the cobblestone makes me jump.

Krampus! I need to get a hold of myself.

The restaurant's bell rings when I enter, and it's followed by Elvis Presley's "Blue Christmas" piping through the speakers. A jukebox sparkles from the corner, and the waitstaff, dressed in vintage uniforms with pointed hats, brush past, carrying platters of hot cakes and other breakfast items to the tables.

I pump myself up mentally. This is going to be a simple and straightforward transaction. No dillydallying, no wayward thoughts of muscles, no banter that could lead to one of our disagreements. We'll switch phones and I'll be on my merry way.

I inform the hostess at the podium that my party is already here and walk toward the booth and Teddy, whose gaze has turned back to the page. He looks so peaceful, so absorbed in his book that he barely notices all the commotion of the restaurant around him.

When I near, Teddy slides out of the booth and stands. The gesture is subtle, done without fanfare, and something in my belly stirs. He smells fresh from the shower, like shampoo and body wash, though I can't detect what brand. Out of the Inn's green sweater, Teddy exudes a different vibe, all loose and languid.

Stop thinking of him like that!

"Hey," he says.

"Hey." There's a frosted glass of ice water at my place setting, and my phone lies faceup next to the rolled-up utensils. I sit down, and he does the same. I peek at the page header of the book he's reading, curiosity nipping at my heels. Whatever it is, does he like it so far? How much does he read?

He closes the book. From a quick glance of the cover, which has a realistic photo of a person climbing a mountain, it looks to be a nonfiction.

Interesting. A book for school? "Whatcha reading?"

"It's about climbing El Capitan. That's a rock formation in Yosemite. But mostly it's about going for a dream, even if it seems far-fetched. I got a great recommendation, so I thought I'd give it a try."

My interest sparks. "A recommendation?"

"Yup." He doesn't look up at me. "Blogger recommendation. Book blogs are how I find my next read."

He reads blogs.

Teddy is truly an onion. With every layer, there's more to discover. Now if only he didn't irritate like one.

Another thought occurs: Why would he even need to tell me that he takes blogger recommendations? Did he snoop into my notifications? Did he read my blog?

"Did you see?"

"See what?" I ask, snapping back to focus, now skeptical. Blogger recommendation, his seemingly relaxed attitude, and this second place setting for me. This is too cordial of an interaction thus far. Did he see me and my friends last night? What's he up to??

He points to a flyer, taped face out against the windowpane he's sitting next to.

I frown and shake my head.

He peels back the paper with nimble fingers and flips it over. On top is the Bookworm Inn logo and, below it, information about New Year's Eve by the Lake.

My suspicions fall back a step with this change of topic. "Oh wow, the news is out."

He points around the restaurant, where the red flyer is taped up in strategic places: on every booth windowpane, the host's podium, and next to the jukebox. In my anticipation, I hadn't even noticed.

"Do you think people will come?" he asks.

"Are you kidding? We're talking about *Holiday by the Lake.*" At the thought of work, I take out his phone from my backpack and hand it to him. Enough small talk. "Anyway . . . here."

He peers at me. "You didn't read my texts, did you?"

"No, of course not!"

"Then where are my notifications?" He thumbs the screen.

"I dunno." Exasperation fills me, and I take back all my positive thoughts about this guy. Serenity doesn't exist here. "Maybe when I answered the phone they went away? Why would I be interested in your texts?"

His expression is both dubious and amused. After a beat of silence, he says, "Hmm."

Hmm? My gut's screaming *He knows something even if he's not saying so.* "Did you check *my* notifications?" My iPhone flashes, and sure enough there are a slew waiting for me. Relief floods me for a beat, but I remember—my notifications only quit showing on the lock screen after I click on them. He could have read them.

"I mean, I couldn't help it," he says.

"So you did!" I yell, then take my volume down when heads turn my way and the waitress sends me a warning look.

"I thought it was my phone at first. Can you blame me? But don't worry, I won't tell anyone that your dad can't figure out what to get your mom for Christmas, or that your sister's mad you took the last bagel. What a mean Ate Lila you are."

If that's all he read, then I'm in the clear. And with no mention of last night, I relax a smidge. Still, the remnants of my flighty, flirty thoughts about Teddy go *whoosh.* "All right, thanks for my phone. I'm out."

"Wanna join me for breakfast? Don't know about you, but I'm starving."

This conversation is like being on a sled on a bumpy hill on an icy, slick day. I have no idea when the next bump and turn will be. "Is this a trick?"

He barks out a laugh. "No. Why would I want to trick you?"

Because you're being too nice right now. "Because you have been a sparkler in my behind since you got here."

His mouth rounds in an O.

I still. Did I just say that? And to the boss's nephew? "I mean—"

"Wow."

"I need to get to school." I slide out of the booth, my cheeks aflame.

"That's too bad." His voice is teasing. "Because I ordered a ton of food."

"Excuse me," says a woman behind me, and I sidestep. The server sets down a large platter of pancakes, sausage, and bacon. "Here's the family-style breakfast and a side of fried marshmallows."

"Thank you, ma'am," he says to her oh so sweetly. "Oooh, and the fried marshmallows. Didn't you want to try them, Lila? It's on your calendar."

I narrow my eyes. The sneak. What else does he know?

The server smiles at him and pats me on the shoulder. "Aren't you staying, hon? I brought out another plate for you."

"Thank you," I answer, though my appetite is nowhere to be

found. I slip back into the seat, fully intending to ignore the food. Even as my mouth begins to water, the traitor.

But he's got me. I can't take off until I know, for sure, what kind of information he has about my blog. I also can't leave him with a bad impression that he can take to Ms. Velasco.

"Now that we got the sparkler bit out of the way." Teddy half laughs, though his expression has tightened.

Guilt settles in. "Teddy, I didn't mean . . . Well, I did . . . but I wish I hadn't said it."

"It's okay." He gestures to the food. "Be my guest."

"I'm not hungry." And yet, my tummy grumbles so loud that the table vibrates. It's the bacon. Me and bacon are like icing to sugar cookies: there's no such thing as too much.

"Sure? I can't finish all of this, and consider it a thanks for bringing my phone to me this morning. And for putting up with my sparkler attitude at work."

My tummy growls again, overshadowing my embarrassment. Reluctantly, I take a piece of bacon and place it onto my plate.

"Look. My feelings aren't hurt, Lila. I know I haven't been, I dunno, excited about working shifts with you. There's just a lot going on right now."

I nod, taking a bite. His honesty endears me to him a smidge, enough that I relax into my seat.

"Wanna try a marshmallow?" he says after he takes a bite of a sausage link. He pushes the plate toward me, and then he grabs a marshmallow, skewered by a short stick, examines it, and slides it off the stick with his teeth.

I do the same. It is an interesting combination of sweet and savory and a crunchy outer shell with gooey insides.

"The verdict? Recommend?"

"Actually, it's not so bad," I say, licking my bottom lip.

"It might be a little too greasy for me." He sips his drink.

In my periphery, the servers gather in a group and stand shoulder to shoulder. When the jukebox track changes to Wham's "Last Christmas," they sing along and do a coordinated dance.

Teddy shakes his head. "Holly is . . ."

"Don't say weird," I warn, my hackles rising.

"You don't think it's odd that this entire city is holidayed out because of one movie?"

"No. Doesn't every place have its quirks? Besides, I live and work here, and so do you, at least for now. It's not such a bad thing, to be around people who lean into the holiday cheer."

He makes a noise.

"Was that . . . was that a grumble? Are you a Scrooge? Is this your shack?" I tease.

"Har-har."

I can't help but smile into my pancakes.

We eat in surprisingly companionable silence sprinkled with small talk. I am famished; perhaps my defensiveness walking into Scrooge's was due to basic morning grumpiness. It was thoughtful of Teddy to order enough food for two, and with no other side comments about my phone, I decide that Teddy doesn't know much more than he's revealed.

Once I've taken the edge off my hunger, his words about my missed texts catch up belatedly.

"So . . . do you have any ideas on what my dad should get for my mom for Christmas?"

He takes another sip of his drink. "Last year my dad gave my mom a mother's necklace. It had a charm of my birthstone. She loved it."

The idea's a good one—Jubilee's Jewels down the street displayed a similar necklace. "I like that, but my parents make it a thing where they set a low budget for their gifts. It's supposed to, quote, 'spark their gifting creativity.' Those are my mom's words. Last year, they capped it at five dollars, and she got him stationery so he could write letters to her. My mom loves getting handwritten notes, and I guess she missed it." The memory makes me smile. Their gift challenge began the year Dad's business closed. It was an especially lean year, and somehow they didn't make a big deal of it.

It might have been one of our best Christmases ever.

"The apple doesn't fall far from the tree," he says.

"What do you mean?"

"Just that you don't miss an opportunity to make a point." His lips curl into an honest-to-goodness grin.

It's a dare, so I challenge him. "Do you mean when I'm right?"

"Exactly." Teddy pauses, like he's come to an idea. "So how would you rate Scrooge's Shack? Five stars or four?" He forks a piece of pancake and examines it.

It's a strange question, but his tone is sincere. "A five. I've eaten here since they opened, at least five years ago. I've never had bad food, not once."

"How about the customer service?"

"Definitely a five. Did you see how fast my powdered sugar showed up?" I peer at him. "Why, are you putting up a review somewhere?"

"Nope. Just wondering."

"Okay?" I scoop another helping onto my plate. With the jukebox in a lull, the brief dead air is deafening. "Next subject. What's your major at Syracuse?" When he shoots me a questioning look, I add, "Ms. Velasco told me."

"Ah." He nods. "Business."

"Do you like the school?"

He shrugs. "It's all core classes right now, so I'm coasting."

"Mmm."

"What's mmm for?"

"Nothing, just that you're so . . ." I wave my fork around and try to work out the description in my head. What's a good description for Teddy that won't insult him? ". . . whatever."

"And you are perhaps . . ."

"*Not* that."

"Ah." He forks another pancake from the platter and drops it onto his plate. "You're a *not that* who takes powdered sugar on her pancakes instead of syrup."

"Which indicates?"

"That there's more to your *not that*."

Now I'm lost. "Is that supposed to be an insult or a compliment?"

He laughs. "It's whatever you want it to be, Lila. It's simply an observation, much like you've made about me. Because I can tell, you don't like me very much."

The way he says this spears me with a lightning bolt of guilt.

"I . . . I don't know why you think that. I haven't done anything to you."

"But you don't agree with the things I ask or do."

"There's a difference between correction and disapproval," I say. "And I correct."

He chews and laughs. "Nope, you disapprove."

"I disagree."

"Okay." He smiles this wide grin that's both disarming and placating all at once. Because we both know that he's made his point—there's no hiding that our personalities aren't in sync. "So what are *you* planning to major in? I bet you applied to ten colleges all early action. With the way you follow my tita's checklists, I bet your life is a spreadsheet."

My face heats—am I that transparent? But at the same time, I'm proud of all I accomplished. Organization is, after all, my strong point. "Eight. But I got into my first choice." I take a sip of my water to clear my thoughts. "Syracuse."

He looks up, eyes crinkling, and he beams. He looks almost as happy as when I saw him at the climbing gym. "Nuh-uh."

"Yep." Pride seeps into my tone. "For bio."

"Huh." He sips his soda.

His reaction is curious, but I go on. "Then hopefully right into medical school."

He nods, still sipping.

"That must be a good drink."

"Oh, ah, yeah." His phone—his actual phone, now that we've swapped back—lights up. It takes all of me not to look at what weird new text he received. Then it buzzes a second and then a third time.

"Do you mind?" He gestures.

"No, go ahead."

He scrolls up and chuckles. Then he glances up for a beat. "Sorry."

"It's okay." I wipe my fingers on my napkin. "Wow, we took that family platter out."

"You're a good restaurant date." His eyes widen. "I mean, not a date, but you know." He clears his throat.

Is that shyness I detect? Whatever it is, it sends my heart into double time, adding to the emotional whiplash of our roller-coaster conversation.

Which means I need to get out of here. This is wrong, all these feelings, whatever they are.

I reach out to grab my phone, but as I do, his hand beats me to it. My hand hovers over his, and though we're not touching, tingles run up my arm.

"Wait. Before you go." His lifts his gaze to me, and I still. Then, slowly he withdraws his hand.

I clear my throat, my gut now screaming at me. "What's up?"

"I wasn't sure how to bring this up. I've been sitting here, thinking that maybe I shouldn't because chilling with you has been okay, but there's no way I can't. Lila, I *know*. And I know that *you* know."

His words are confusing, to say the least. I frown. "What you just said was a whole lot of *I knows,* but not much else. I've no idea what you're talking about."

He grabs his soda glass and wipes the condensation with a thumb, his jaw muscle working.

In the silence I wonder: How does one get a jaw muscle? Does he do jaw exercises when he tones his shoulders and back muscles? Was that something he built up slowly at the climbing gym?

"Are you listening?" Teddy's eyebrows are raised.

"No." Shaking my head, I try again. "I mean, I don't get it. You're going to have to give me a little bit more to go on."

He sighs. "You aren't sly, Santos. I saw you and your friends at the climbing gym. Spying."

Tiny microbeads of sweat build up at my temples. "What climbing gym?"

His eyeballs roll back for a beat. "The one you went to last night."

"Mmm." I tap my chin to distract myself. Because distraction is the key while I try to sort out my alibi. "Last night? Nope. Not me."

He sighs. "The three of you were hard to miss."

"Still don't know what you're talking about."

"So we're going to pretend. All right." He sits up. "Look, you can't tell anyone that I was there. Not a soul, especially not Tita Lou."

Interesting.

Here's the thing about being a big sister. I can see through the fluff and slight panic. Teddy is desperate, which means that there's something to tell. And seeing him stress is vindication.

Then again, why would I care?

I reel back my thoughts to square one. "For the record, I was not spying."

"Lila . . . okay, fine." He pinches the bridge of his nose. "But don't tell Tita Lou. Please."

My tummy flip-flops at his distress. I might be big-sister bossy, but I'm not mean. "Fine, fine, I won't."

"Thank you." He exhales.

"But can I ask why?"

"I'd rather you not. It's complicated." He avoids my eyes.

"All right." I don't push it. As far as I'm concerned, we're even. The switch is complete. Time to move on.

He breathes out a sigh. "God, I was getting myself ready. I thought I was going to need to bring out the big guns."

"The big guns?" Warning bells sound off in my head. "Wait . . . When you said '*I know*' . . ."

Teddy changes positions, leaning back and steepling his fingers. His previously working jaw muscle relaxes into a mischievous grin.

My heart speeds up in turn. "Teddy?"

"I was just going to say . . . I'm glad that I didn't have to resort to bringing up your anonymous blog to convince you to keep my secret quiet."

It's a plot twist that brings me to the edge of my seat, and I accidentally nudge the table. Water sloshes out of my cup. "I . . . I don't—"

Teddy raises a hand, and he's smiling—the gall of him. "Before you deny it, I have my own sleuthing skills, and it was easy enough to find you, Ms. Tinsel and Tropes. I thought I'd read enough book blogs, but you . . . God, you have hundreds of posts. I didn't realize there were so many holiday books. How many do you read a week?"

My shock at being caught runs headlong into my pride. I shake my head. "It's not important. And I'm not sure why you're bringing my blog into it, because I don't even care about your so-called secret. Why does it matter if people know? It's climbing. It's a sport."

"It's not just a sport. It is the perfect combination of being free and also taking control." The way he talks about it brings a light to his face, so unlike what he shows at the Inn. But his expression crashes down with his next words. "But all that matters is that you stay quiet. You don't spill my secret, and I won't spill yours. Got it?"

Teddy isn't asking me now; he's telling me. The leftover taste of that fried marshmallow goes sour. I slide my phone into my back pocket and retrieve my wallet. I throw down a ten on the table with an obnoxious flourish. "Whatever. Like I care. Got it."

Chapter 10

It's complicated.

Teddy's words echo in my mind as I enter the gift shop's back doors and head right into the break room, to the set of lockers for part-time staff. Today is my and Teddy's second training day together, and after yesterday's disastrous meal at Scrooge's, I'm dreading seeing him.

And when I open my usual locker, it's already in use. A sweatshirt is balled up on the bottom, and atop is a key ring with at least five carabiners. Obviously Teddy's things.

"Really?" I grumble. It's not enough that he blackmailed me?

"Lila." KC walks in with a surprised look on his face. "You're working today?"

"Yeah, it's my second day with Teddy. His shift started earlier with Ms. Velasco, and I'm taking over to train. But look! He took my locker. Everyone, everyone, everyone knows this is my locker." But as soon as I say the words, I deflate a little. "Sorry, I know I sound like a brat."

"No sweat. I'm off now, so you can take my locker." KC fiddles with his lock and pulls it open. He grabs his backpack and gives me a side-eye. "Are you okay? I wasn't sure after your last text."

He's referencing my text update after my breakfast with Teddy yesterday: *It went okay. I have my phone.*

"It's fine. Everything's fine." I repeat what I told Carm when she followed up yesterday at school. She gave me a hard time about having fried marshmallows without her.

"You don't sound fine."

I sigh. Explaining everything would just open a can of worms—*secret* worms—so I regroup. "I am, really, I swear." I offer a smile.

"Well." He winces. "You might find a couple of things amiss out there."

"Okay." I stuff my things in KC's locker, and his foreboding tone catches up to me. Teddy saw not only me, but also KC and Carm at the climbing gym last night. And now he holds my deepest secret. "Teddy—has he, um, said anything to you?"

"About what?" An eyebrow lifts.

The moment is saved by buzzing and KC fishes his phone out. My shoulders drop with relief. This is becoming complicated, all right.

He beams. "It's Seb. His flight's early. I've got to head out."

"I'm glad he's coming back for the holidays."

"Me too." A smile melts onto his face. "But anyway, I've got to run. Just . . ." He heads to the doorway. "Just breathe, okay?"

"Okay?" I half laugh. "Have fun with Seb."

"Oh, and . . ." He points to a new corkboard display on the wall before he disappears around the doorway. "New info."

I gaze up at the corkboard, now labeled *New Year's Eve at the*

Lake. Tacked below it are sheets of paper, all labeled with necessary tasks and assignments. I take a quick pic of them to review later.

Also posted is a copy of the flyer that I saw at Scrooge's that will be used to advertise on our social media. There's a Post-it stuck in front of it that says, *Tickets went on sale this morning, now twenty-five percent full. Detailed schedule will go up soon.*

Whoa. I quickly text my mom: *Don't forget to buy two tickets to New Year's Eve by the Lake. Filling up quick!*

Mom: *Got it!*

Below the flyer is a sign-up list for the employee lottery to determine who's going to work the event. A pencil hangs on a string next to it, and, no surprise, most of the staff has written their names. I add mine, too, just in case tickets sell out before Mom can snag a couple.

As I walk out onto the gift shop floor, I imagine myself working the New Year's Eve event. The shop will be packed like wet snow, with Michael Bublé on full throttle. Then the music will cut out and the iconic *Holiday by the Lake* theme song will play, and Jonah and Remy will walk in. Remy will recognize me as her all-time fan and sign my program, and I'll have the thrill of meeting someone who looks like me and who has made it.

In real life, at the moment, the gift shop has barely a dozen people in it—slower than usual. To my right, Teddy is wiping down the windows with a rag, a sign that he's following Ms. Velasco's maintenance checklist. Which is good, because the less I have to speak to him, the better. My goal for today: keep shoving lists and tasks in front of him until our shift is over. The more things to do, the faster time will pass where I have to be in close proximity to Teddy and his threats.

"Hi, Lila." Cliff, another part-timer passes me. Against his chest, he's carrying replica oars for the canoe. He juggles it with precision as he says, "The library looks great. So many people have picked up books."

"Um, thanks." Except, I haven't done anything to it since the last time I was here.

Then I remember Teddy, the other day, shelving my books.

I hustle around the corner. To the spines now arranged by color.

"Oh. My. God." My mouth drops open at the sight of the rainbow spines. On my shelves. Of my library.

Even more: there are six people in front of these shelves, enamored, taking books out to read the back covers. Several have a book or two under their arms.

My heart leaps. I have never seen this many people in front of my shelves at any given time. At most, one, maybe two people are drawn to this corner space.

Right now, it really does look so pretty.

This was the library's goal. This is Tinsel and Tropes's goal. To bring people together with books.

But I spot the spine of a travel book next to a novel. A mystery next to a romance. All of the books are mixed together. Classics with travel, fiction with nonfiction, children's with adults.

KC's words echo in my mind: *Just breathe.*

"Surprise!" Teddy appears at my side, both hands on his hips and a satisfied, proud smile on his face.

I, on the other hand, am frozen in place. "You did this?"

"Yep. It was slow this morning, and so I thought why not? It's such a good look."

"That is definitely a look. But." Slowly, my reaction forms

under my skin—it's frustration. Anger. But customers and staff are milling about; I can't blow up. With the steadiest voice I can muster, I say, "It's all wrong. And you did it without asking me."

"I . . . I mean, yeah, it's not alphabetical or by genre. But does that make it wrong? Look how many people like it. I thought you would too." His tone is hopeful—it is quite the opposite of his smugness at Scrooge's.

He's right; these people do love it.

He thinks he's helping me.

But has he forgotten? He knows about my blog and he's holding it against me to protect his own secret. Now he's trying to encroach on my space.

I take a deep breath and look away. To a T-shirt display that's half empty. And to the box of lights sitting next to the registers— all tasks on Ms. Velasco's to-do list. "You should be focusing on your own work, your own issues, not mine."

His eyes flash, understanding that I'm talking about more than these shelves. "Geesh. I'm sorry. I'll fix it back," he says quickly, leaning in as if we're in cahoots. "I was checking out all the book bloggers on Instagram and so many of them had rainbow spines and—"

"Shhh," I snap, and look around for anyone within hearing distance. Doesn't he know what it means to keep a secret? "Forget about it. I'll fix it back." Then, despite Teddy's hurt expression— and why should I even care that *he's* hurt—I spin on my heel and put space between me and him, before I can say anything else I might regret.

During the first half of my shift with Teddy, while I'm still brood-ing over the rainbow bookshelves, I try to instruct him on how to sort the hoodies against the back wall (customers prefer it when we sort by size rather than by color) and the importance of play-ing the movie playlist over the surround sound versus today's pop-ular music (we want customers to buy the CD from us). All to a myriad of Teddy's objections.

For the most part I'm able to keep my frustrations in check. Through gritted teeth, I dig deep to unearth my holiday cheer that Teddy somehow smothers whenever he is around.

That is, until I see him rolling the T-shirts instead of using the T-shirt folder as instructed—and I turn into the Abominable Snowman. As soon as there are no more customers at the register, I stalk toward him with a roar building in my chest.

"Let me guess, you have a problem with how I'm doing my job," he says before I'm able to speak. "And you want me to use the T-shirt folder. But these T-shirts are on sale, and I've been back and forth twice today to stock it. Why not fit more by roll-ing a few and stacking them up?" He finishes what looks like a pyramid of T-shirts and presents it like a prize. "Voilà."

It's a good idea. I know it's a good idea. But Teddy neither asked nor did he communicate these changes to me or anyone else in the gift shop. Again. "Teddy, the way to a customer's heart is through their eyes. And rolling the T-shirts makes them look like they're only good enough to camp in. You can't even see the graphic on the shirt." I hold out the shirt-folding contraption to him.

Two hours. A short two hours left in this shift, and then I can go home and tunnel into a book that will be an escape portal from these last couple of days.

His expression hardens. "Seriously?"

"Would it kill you?"

"Would it hurt to try something new? I thought for sure you would be open to some creativity around here. The lists, the display. The library. Why isn't there any give?"

The question has too many layers to unpack. Where should I start? Because I'm simply enforcing the rules? That maybe, if it's good enough, then don't fix it? And who is he to make changes in the first place?

But I don't want to argue. I don't have the space to argue. I can barely even wrap my mind around our conversation at Scrooge's. So, instead, I shake the T-shirt folder in front of his face. "Please, use it." I glance back at the register, where triplet girls have approached, each with the Inn's signature ornament—a glass book. "Take it."

Finally, with a quiet and protracted sigh, he gently accepts the contraption.

"Thank you. After you're done here, we have a couple of things to do for the New Year's Eve event. Ms. Velasco bought white Christmas trees to place at every corner of the shop. We'll need to put all four up, along with lights." I step away. Behind me, Teddy mumbles something indiscernible.

I turn around, raise my eyebrows at him.

He lifts his hands up, as if innocent. But by the look on his face, I can bet what he said wasn't innocent at all.

At my and Teddy's assigned break, I rush ahead of him to the break room so I can grab my book and coat for alone time outside.

I kept it together most of the shift. After our T-shirt non-argument, which I won, we kept out of each other's way. He's gotten the hang of most tasks at the register, which gave me the opportunity to brainstorm my blog post for *Menorah Mayhem* while putting up two of the white trees.

I mess with the lock of the locker and pull my backpack out. When I turn, Teddy is walking in, and he raises a finger and opens his mouth to speak, but I brush past him. "Not in the mood, Teddy."

I won't let him occupy every bit of my life. It's bad enough I have to worry about my secret getting out.

Except by the time I settle into my chair, it starts to snow and flakes are sticking to my screen. I shut my laptop and, despite the cold, pull out my next read, the second book in the Hanukkah Hijinks cozy mystery series.

Diving into a book, even for ten minutes, usually resets my day. Not only does reading calm me, but oftentimes books put things in perspective. Stories remind me that there's more to my surroundings. Reading helped me through those out-of-control feelings when Dad lost his shop. I never leaned on my free library more than the time when we couldn't afford books.

But this time, when I look at the book in my lap, all I can think of is what Teddy said in the gift shop.

I thought for sure you would be open to some creativity around here.

I am creative, aren't I? I write. I work on my blog design and change it up as much as I can. And I read. I read so much and get so immersed in stories that I sometimes think of characters as people—I hurt when they're in pain and swoon when they fall in love.

But the world isn't made of creativity alone. There are rules, after all. And do I have to be creative all the time? Can't I just enjoy this . . . work . . . separately?

Finally, who is he to judge any part of me, my creativity, my secrets, when he has his own issues to sort through? I didn't ask to be roped into his family drama. And now, somehow, I'm inextricably linked to Teddy when all I ever really wanted were more work hours.

Anger pulses through me. It's what I've been repressing throughout my shift.

I'm on my feet before I can register my body moving. While I still have to protect my own secret, it doesn't mean I should have to keep silent about my discontent. I might have not objected after he trapped me into his secret, but I don't have to make things easy for him. I throw the door open and step in, and the whoosh of warm air is a catalyst to my rising temper. When I enter the break room, I'm ready to tell Teddy off.

I'm also ready to inform Ms. Velasco that her worst employee is her nephew.

Teddy's sitting at the table wearing earbuds, and his gaze lifts from his phone screen to me. He straightens and takes out an earbud. "Listen, Lila. Honestly, I didn't mean to tick you off this badly."

"I . . . what?" I reel back, stunned. I was all prepared to let him know where he could stick his candy cane.

"I feel like I need to explain more about . . . stuff." He lowers his voice, his gaze over my shoulder, as another Bookworm Inn employee passes by. "Are you free tomorrow night, by chance?"

"What more do you have to explain?"

"About climb—"

Ms. Velasco's voice filters through the hallway, and she appears at the break room doorway, head thrown back in a cackle, with a person I don't recognize.

"Hi, you two," she says in a singsong voice. "This is Kira Mahoney. She's the PR rep for Jonah Johanson."

I do a double take. Someone from Jonah Johanson's camp? "Oh my gosh. Nice to meet you."

Kira is a Black woman and is wearing a ribbed turtleneck with a puffy vest. Her short hair is trimmed into a layered pixie cut and iridescent sunglasses perch on her head. She, too, has a huge smile on her face.

Suddenly everyone's smiling, even Teddy.

"Kira was just in town . . . ," Ms. Velasco starts.

Kira continues. "I was driving through. My family lives in Rochester, and I thought, why not stop by and do a once-over of the place to prep for Jonah? Lou and I have been in communication for a while now."

"Months," Ms. Velasco says.

"Four months." She glances at Ms. Velasco with a grin. "I'm glad we finally get to meet."

"Thank you for writing me back."

"Months, huh?" Teddy asks, right eyebrow wiggling. I see what Teddy sees: Ms. Velasco and Kira are standing close, and the darkened cheeks that I thought were from the cold look more like blushes.

It's a scene out of a rom-com, and it hits me like one. A giggle threatens to burst from my lips.

"Anyway, I just wanted to introduce you all. We have a lot of things to cover. I'm showing Kira the grounds and the conference room," Ms. Velasco says. "Have a good break, you two."

"Nice to meet you," I say as Ms. V and Kira exit, already deep in chatter.

I bite my lip and turn to Teddy. He's beaming. "Do you think?" I ask.

"I don't know?" he says. "It's been forever since . . ."

I've seen her with anyone.

His gaze drops to the table just as I complete the sentence in my head. Ms. Velasco is mostly business, so sometimes I forget that she lives alone. She had a partner years ago, though their relationship ended by the time I started working at the Inn.

"Well, I hope that she . . ." Except I don't really know what I want to say. Ms. Velasco is the epitome of the kind of person I want to be—ambitious, successful.

I've always thought that work makes a person. That working solves it all.

But does it?

Once again, my head is jumbled.

My phone alarm rings in my back pocket, and it refocuses me.

"Our break's up," I say, thankful for the distraction. I don't want to spend any more time with a person who's threatening to expose Tinsel and Tropes. I stuff my backpack into the locker and head to the front.

Title: Menorah Mayhem (Hanukkah Hijinks #1) by Liz Zimmerman
CATEGORY/GENRE: COZY MYSTERY

Is it really a secret if other people know?

Set during Hanukkah, *Menorah Mayhem* is about a protagonist with a secret and an organization with a secret, all surrounding the mysterious disappearance of the town's menorah sculpture. Told from the detective's point of view, the book soon reveals that most everyone in the town was somewhat involved.

It begs the discussion: What classifies a secret? So, I looked up the definition. According to the *Merriam-Webster Dictionary*, a secret means "kept from knowledge or view."

In this case, if everyone knows the secret, then where's the conflict? And why would a reader want to hang on until the very last page when everyone seems to be in on it?

Here's your answer: Because it's so well written! This book shows that while everyone's keeping the same secret, their motivations for keeping the secret set them apart. It's their motivations that conflict! And the tropes! Kidnapping, blackmail, and revenge are tropes that usually belong in a dark book. But cozy mysteries can balance between crime and humor. In this story, with Hanukkah added to the mix, this book skews more toward fun and celebration. I can't say much more than that without spoiling it.

One thing I will reveal: This book ends in a cliffhanger. If you are anti-cliffhanger like I am (see my About Me page here), then I am doing you a huge favor by warning you ahead of time.

Cliffhangers should be banned.

Still, you should read it. I certainly am now clamoring for the second book.

Are you pro- or anti-cliffhanger?

Pros: I really like the protagonist, and the cover is so pretty!

Cons: Did we really need two hundred and fifty pages if it all ends in a cliffhanger? Cliffhangers shouldn't be allowed.

Recommended for: Those who are tolerant of cliffhangers.

Rating: 4 stars!

Chapter 11

I wake up to about twenty-five comments on my last blog post, all on my lock screen notifications. After scanning them through bleary eyes and discerning they're the usual suspects, I decide to respond to them after school. I never like to rush through responding to comments—bookworms always have such great things to say.

I crawl out of bed, careful to avoid treading on Irene, who had another one of her vivid dreams. She can't fall back asleep after she wakes up from one, and at least once a month she drags her blanket and pillow next to me, first on the bed when we were much younger and smaller, and now on the floor.

Today is the last half day before school ends for winter break. I cannot wait to be able to sleep in.

I pad into the kitchen, where I turn on lights and turn off the exhaust vent light—it's our night-light for anyone who wanders into the kitchen—and make my oatmeal, start the coffee, and bring out cups for my parents, an automatic thing. It's one of those lessons they taught us: bring out yours, bring out others' too. Mom should be walking into the house soon from her night shift, and Dad's probably in the shower.

Sure enough, moments later, Mom pushes open the back door. The cold wafts in with her bright smile. "Iha. How sweet!" she says as she kicks off her clogs. After hanging her coat, she steps into the laundry room to get into her robe, which she keeps right at the entrance, and washes her hands so she doesn't bring in germs from the hospital.

"And timely." Dad enters, smelling like his cologne, and kisses me on the forehead. His chin is smooth, unlike at the end of the day, when his five-o'clock shadow is as rough as pine tree needles. He's wearing his That's A Wrap polo, with a name tag lanyard blinged out with pins.

"You're tired." Mom's turn to kiss me, this time on the cheek. She examines me like I'm one of her patients. "You're working too hard. What time did you come home last night?"

"The Aguilers didn't get back from their date until eleven. So I didn't come home until almost midnight, and I couldn't sleep until about one."

Mr. and Mrs. Aguiler are what you call the young couple type. They have three kids under the age of five—Micah, Dustin, and Penelope—who I babysit about every two weeks. When the two go out, it's not just for a quiet dinner—they party like they'd been caged animals in a zoo. They come home sweaty and red-faced, and the PDA is over the top and embarrassing. Who wants to see the people you work for nuzzle into one another? (Not me!) It's so different from how my parents are, who are chaste in public and even around us kids.

They love their privacy in all forms.

"Thought I heard you typing on your computer late last night," Dad says pointedly. He's a light sleeper.

I grit my teeth and brace myself for the next question.

Mom holds her coffee cup to her lips. "I hope you didn't spend all that time online. I don't like it when you . . . what do they call it? Doomscroll?"

"I wasn't doomscrolling, Mom, and no, I wasn't online."

Because technically I was working on my blog post offline before I cut and pasted it to the dashboard.

"We know you're eighteen, but—"

"Mom. Please." We've had this conversation countless times before, and it's only seven in the morning.

"Psht. Don't talk back to your mother." Dad takes a sip of his coffee with a grin.

It's the role we play. Mom lays down the law, and Dad pretends to back her up, when he's really just trying to stay out of trouble himself.

I mumble, "I'm sorry." Because I *am* sorry that I got caught. Also, by apologizing, she'll drop the subject. When I'm working my normal hours at the Inn, I can reliably write up my blog posts at the gift shop. But now my schedule's a mess with Teddy's training plugged in haphazardly. So, my room has to be it.

Thinking about Teddy reminds me of his weird request, that we should get together to talk. Whatever that means.

I feel a gentle pressure against my ear. Mom is pulling at my bedhead strands of hair and tucking them back. "I'm sorry. It's just that we worry. It doesn't mean we don't trust you. It's because I want to protect you. And online . . . it's messy out there."

"Mom, I think I've been online longer than you."

"I know." Her gaze darts up to Dad, then back to my face.

"But it doesn't make it less impactful. I know it's not all bad. There's good in it for sure, but I worry that if you get lost in it, well . . . just be mindful of your choices about what to share and when. Privacy is still very important."

She doesn't have to say the rest. I don't want her to, because what we both know, and what Dad knows better than anyone, is that, for our family, the internet has brought more bad than good.

But my blog is different. First of all, it's anonymous, and secondly, it's so small that no one even knows it exists. And my blog gives me a way to express my emotions, even if it's simply my thoughts around a book.

Still, I don't argue because there's no point. Eventually, Mom yawns and heads upstairs to rouse the rest of the family.

Dad grabs his coat. "I'm off." He gives me another kiss on the forehead. "Good luck with finals today. Are you working tonight?"

"No. It's a Mission: Holly night."

"Good. You need a break." He takes a few steps and slaps his flat cap on his head. "By the way, thanks for your idea on a mom's necklace. I ended up finding an alternative."

"Yeah? What is it?"

"You're going to have to see." He grins and takes a step toward the door, then turns back to face me. "Iha, we talk a lot about privacy but it really boils down to choosing how much you want to share. It's hard enough to figure out what you want without the peanut gallery. We want you to have that opportunity to do it without pressure, or without consequences from strangers." He gives me a final kiss on the forehead. "Okay?"

I nod with a sigh. Then I'm alone in the kitchen, with the

sounds of my younger siblings stirring upstairs, and the thought that has occupied my head for a while now: What *do* I want, anyway?

"That was confusing as heck." Carm shuffles behind me out of AP Bio. "I got all of my hand and arm muscles all mixed up. How'd you do? Let me guess. Just fine?"

"Totally fine." I grin. We walk side by side toward our lockers, and I'm feeling light on my toes. I killed that exam.

"Curse you," she grumbles.

I laugh. "Don't ask me how I did in statistics, though."

"True, true."

We get to our lockers, with hers just a shout's distance from mine.

"Ready for tonight?" she asks.

"Comet's Cider, here we come!" I answer with mild sarcasm as I stuff my books into my locker, then slam the door shut and grin. To be honest, doughnuts sound like a great way to end the semester.

Ta-ta until the new year, textbooks.

I check my notifications. A new comment was posted a couple of hours ago, and instead of one or two sentences, there's simply a link. The comment is from Santa with a View.

Anonymous commenters aren't out of the blue, but randomly sent links are, so I click on it. It sends me to BookGalley, a book review site. They have an open call for interns.

"I think we should commit all the way by not only having cider doughnuts but also hot apple cider drinks. And what's the point of me talking if you're not listening." Carm's voice dials up as she advances toward me, punctuated with a sigh.

"Sorry." I look up, catching the tail end of what she said.

She laughs. "What's up?"

"I was linked to this call for an internship." I hand Carm my phone.

"Who's Santa with a View?"

"I have no idea."

She scrolls. "This internship is totally up your alley. Are you going to apply?"

"Should I?"

"I mean, why not?" We make our way outside, slinging our puffy coats over our shoulders.

"Oh, I don't know, let's see . . . um, that I would reveal who I am?" I shake my head, half laughing. "My parents will find out that I've been lying all this time."

She shrugs. "I don't think it's as bad as you think it's going to be."

"And I should be looking for an internship in my future career, shouldn't I? Why would it help for me to do this, if, by pure chance, I get picked?"

She shivers as a gust of wind cuts through the air. "Because writing is what you do. And you're so good at this."

She says it with such ease that it stuns me. Since sophomore year I have been focused on getting As and participating in every extracurricular activity so I can get into Syracuse for bio, and then to med school. Being a doctor is all I've talked about becoming. "Writing is just a hobby."

"A hobby that you've been committed to for forever." We step off the curb, then cross to the high school parking lot. The slots are numbered and her car is parked in the opposite direction. "You should apply. Besides, who says you need to choose now?"

"It's called a major. I applied under bio."

"All right, fine, but you're just turning in an application. Who knows, right?"

"Who knows," I echo. Those words prove my point. Changing my path right now will only lead to a winding road, and if I was given an internship at BookGalley, my focus would stray from the straight path to success. Add the fact that my parents would be furious that I'd broken their rules of no social media for two years and counting. Yes, I'm eighteen now, but I wasn't when I began Tinsel and Tropes. It is a breach of their trust—something I joke around about but that, on the inside, I'm serious about never wanting to lose.

Carm looks at her phone and sighs. "Cripes. My dad just texted. He made reservations for dinner." She sticks her bottom lip out. "We have to reschedule cider doughnuts."

I frown. "Bummer."

"I'm sorry. But when the parentals call . . ."

"If anyone knows this rule, I do."

"I'll let KC know, and I'll put another date on the calendar, 'kay?" She walks backward, shivering.

I nod. "All right."

Steps away, her voice trills in the cold air. "Fill out that application!"

When I climb into my car, my phone buzzes with a text. "Okay, I heard you." My friend, if anything, is persistent.

But when I check the screen, it's not Carm, but from a number I don't recognize.

It's Teddy. Can we talk?

Lila: How are you texting me?

Teddy: I called my phone from
yours the other day, remember?
What are you doing tonight?

Lila: Stuff

Teddy: I need to see you. Please.

I gape at the word *need.*

What follows is the vision of shirtless Teddy climbing. Heat
climbs up my neck in a sudden rush, and I push the thought away
and stomp it down with my imaginary boots.

I can't think of him this way, not in the slightest bit.

First of all, while I'm all about crushes and book boyfriends,
real ones have no room in my schedule. And second, this is Teddy.
Teddy who I clash with. Who blackmailed me.

Lila: What do you need that you can't text?

Teddy: This needs to be said in person.
The train depot. 7pm?

Lila: Bossy much?

Teddy: 7pm then

I frown, intrigued. He's serious. This must be about his secret, and therefore, mine.

> **Lila:** Okay

Something is up with Teddy Rivera, and I don't know if I can wait till seven to find out what that is.

Chapter 12

The train depot is a highly sought after location in Holly for pictures, and today, a group of tourists jam themselves in front of the depot sign, all wearing various ugly Christmas sweaters. I stand at the corner, far enough away not to accidentally photobomb their selfies, but close enough so their voices reach my ears.

Half of them are complaining:

"I should be the one in front since I'm the shortest."

"It's so cold—who thought this was a good idea?"

"Ugh, this thing is itchy."

"I'm so tired. How long are we staying out here?"

The people smile through gritted teeth. Some with cocked hips, others with dipped shoulders. Before my eyes, I imagine this scene transforming into reality TV drama. One of them says something uncouth, a little too loudly. Another acts shocked at the other's bad behavior. Someone takes off their scarf to defend their alliances, another removes their blinking Christmas balls earrings and—

"Lila."

I spin; Teddy's a foot away from me. He's wearing a puffy coat, and a knit cap covers his head, though wisps of his dark hair peek out from underneath. He's holding two to-go cups and hands me one.

"Oh, wow." Surprised, I accept the cup stamped with the delicate gold-outlined logo of Blitzen Chocolates. It's warm even through the paper sleeve and my knit gloves. Steam escapes from the tiny hole on the cover, and all at once my mouth waters. Hot chocolate—my favorite. "That's . . . You didn't have to."

"I know. But it's one of the things on the list of things to do in Holly."

"That's right, you know," I grunt.

"I looked up the entire list. Can we sit over there? Might as well check off number nine while we're here." He gestures to a hidden table behind the depot, which is remarkably free, painted with the alternate black and white squares of a chessboard top, with chess pieces set upon it randomly.

I sit down and cross one leg over the other, both hands around the cup. I'm warmed by Teddy's thoughtfulness for this entire outing, despite my best efforts to stay mad and suspicious over why we're here in the first place. "So . . . what's up?"

"I wanted to . . ." The last of his words is overtaken by the sound of the trolley's bells. I look to the right; it rolls by, carrying singing carolers, some hanging from its entrance.

"Excuse me . . . what?"

"I said I'm sorry," he shouts.

My mouth hangs agape. Teddy has never, ever apologized or acted remorseful, in all the days I've known him. (Which, okay, has only been about a week.) As the singing carolers fade in the distance, he leans slightly forward in his seat.

"The way I acted yesterday, pitting your secret with mine—I

was a little overzealous. And honestly, I can't keep working like this, with you angry at me. Yesterday was tense."

A snowflake flickers down to the top of the chessboard. "You blackmailed me."

He nods gravely. "That wasn't my good side. I didn't know what to do."

Call me a pushover—I read once that reading teaches people empathy—but in this moment, I feel for Teddy. "I would have kept the secret for you, you know. Even if you are . . ." I pause, mulling over my words.

"Stubborn?"

"At least. More like infuriating."

He throws his head back in a laugh. "Don't hold back now."

I grit my teeth into a smile.

"I do appreciate your honesty. You might not believe it, but you have been one of the best parts of this break."

I cough into my cup. "You're right, I don't believe it. You called me your nemesis."

His eyebrows lift in surprise. "Oh my God. You read that?"

"I did."

He winces. "I guess I did say that. I was intimidated by you at first. You're so . . . on it. But that was before I realized how on it you are with everything. Straightforward. Hardworking. Honest. It makes me want to be honest with you too." He readjusts his knit cap. "I'm starting to get tired of keeping it a secret from everyone."

I swirl my hot chocolate in the cup to distract myself from my growing curiosity.

"There's a bouldering competition the third of January. It's for newbs like me."

"You didn't look like a newb."

"It only looks impressive to those who don't climb, but I'm very new. The competition is why I'm here, in Holly. Climb Holly is sponsoring the event. I asked Tita Lou to take me in for the winter. I made it seem like I needed a job and wanted to work instead of heading back to California, where I would have just ended up sitting on my butt—though I do need a job to pay for the climbing."

As a reader, I detect a crater-size plot hole, like why does this need to be a secret at all? But the conversation feels serious. And I'm not going to push it; keeping his secret is easy enough to do.

"I guess you're excused, then," I say.

"For what?"

"For taking my hours this winter." But as soon as the words leave my mouth, I regret it immediately.

"Oh. Oh dang. I'm sorry." Sincerity bleeds in his tone. "I had no idea."

"Don't say that. I hate that."

"What?"

"Pity." Again, I'm shocked at what I'm saying. Either the hot chocolate or Teddy has loosened my tongue.

"It's not pity. Just . . . sorry. I didn't mean . . ." Then he half laughs. "*That's* why you're even more upset when I don't do what you ask. It explains the fire you're always laying down on me."

For some reason, the thought of me as fire sparks joy. A smile worms its way onto my lips.

"Now you're just being smug."

I laugh. "No, you're right. It might explain that tirade the other day."

He winces. "I deserved it."

I shrug.

"See? That's fire." Teddy sits up. "Thanks for keeping my secret. This competition—it means a lot to me."

His gaze is so intense that I look down at my hot chocolate. Suddenly I feel this need to share too. "When you said that you're starting to get tired of keeping secrets—I get that."

"Yeah?"

"Yeah. My blog. I'm at this point where . . ." I'm not sure where I'm going with my train of thought, with the internship application on my mind and the second anniversary coming up, so I heave a breath. "I feel like I'm in a little bit of a limbo."

"Limbo with your blog? It's pretty awesome in my opinion."

"You think?"

He nods. "It's why I asked you about premed. You know, at Scrooge's? The vibe I get from you is that you'd be a writer. Not to say that you wouldn't do well at anything else."

"It's not practical to be a writer. That's just time-tested. My mother's a nurse, and she has never gone without a job. She pulled us through when . . ." I think about how to frame my family history so that it's not saying too much. I'm not ashamed of what happened, but I don't want my family to be judged, ever. ". . . things were rough. I will always have writing. I don't have to lose it."

"True. But there's only so much time during the day, and shouldn't you be doing something that you enjoy?"

"That's a privilege, though, isn't it?"

In my head, there is a true delineation between premed Lila and blogger Lila. Saying this out loud to Teddy, however, I realize

I actually didn't think this all the way through. Once college begins, will I have to let go of blogger Lila? Will there be time to blog? Will I be limiting myself if I choose one or the other?

"I still don't get why you're keeping it a secret," he says.

"It's my parents. They've got . . . rules."

"They're strict?"

"No, I wouldn't even say that." I bite my lip. What happened with That's A Wrap could easily be Googled, but the repercussions run deep, and it's not all my story to tell. And to complain about it doesn't give credence to how serious the harassment and doxing truly was.

Teddy and I are having a good moment, but it doesn't mean I trust him a hundred percent.

"It's complicated," I finally say.

"All right. Well. Your secret is safe with me." He reaches out a gloved hand, as if to shake mine. "Truce?"

I take it. "Truce."

He leans forward, his grin wicked. "Good. Because I may end up needing you, Santos."

I pretend-frown at his playful tone. "Oh?"

"I have to practice. A lot. And unfortunately for me, I might have to skip out on work. Fortunately for you, there might be hours for you to pick up, if you don't mind. I'd love it if . . ."

"Yes." I nod. "I'll take those hours in a heartbeat."

"Good." He sips his hot chocolate, eyes on my face. They crinkle at the corners, and the heaviness I felt coming here to the train depot evaporates. "So . . . since you're so good at sparring with me, want to go all the way?"

My voice hitches in my throat. "What??"

He reaches forward so his fingers hover nearby, then grabs the black chess pieces from my side of the board.

"Oh . . . chess."

"Yeah. What did you think I meant?" He smiles and pushes the white pieces across the board to me. "Wait. You're not a chess whiz on the DL, are you? I can't have you quartering me like marshmallows and putting me in your hot chocolate."

I raise my eyes to meet his. *Oh my God.*

"What?" he asks.

"Teddy Rivera, did you make a holiday metaphor?"

"No, I—" He brings the cup to his lips. "All right, all right. This place has gotten to me, okay? Yesterday, I slipped on the ice and said 'holy night.' Holy. Night! I mean—" He laughs into his cup.

I crack up at the thought.

"Oh, man." I wipe the side of my eyes. "That's good. That's really good."

He digs a hand into his coat pocket, still chuckling, and retrieves his buzzing phone. "Sorry, I have to get this. Hello? Hey, Mom." His smile dims a smidge. He turns away, as if hiding himself.

I twist in the other direction, too, to give him privacy, and tamp down my ever-growing curiosity about Teddy. I click the e-reader app on my phone. Once again, I thank the heavens above for technology; it makes it a million times easier to escape.

"Yeah, things are okay here. I'm totally fine, Mom," Teddy whispers.

Except I can't seem to focus with Teddy speaking in these hushed, sweet tones.

"Of course I'm staying safe. I'm fine," he continues. "You guys enjoy. Yes. I'll take more pictures. Did you? No, I didn't see that comment. Okay. Love you. Yes. Okay. Tell Dad I love him too."

I bite the inside of my lip at the cuteness of it all. It adds an extra layer to my confusion, at the family drama Ms. Velasco hinted at, and the rest of Teddy's secret.

"Sorry about that," he says, placing the last of his chess pieces in the right squares. "So, are you ready? While you hustle me in chess, I can tell you all about Syracuse life."

After a beat, I say, truthfully, "As I'll ever be."

Chapter 13

When I arrive at work the next day for my last training shift with Teddy, a new list is posted on the break room corkboard.

Employees working the New Year's Eve at the Lake event.

I charge straight for the list. As I run a finger down the letter-size paper, Teddy bounds in with a groan. "Dang, it's cold out there."

I press a finger against the list to keep my place. His hair is dotted with gigantic snowflakes. They're the soft kind, not wet enough for snowmen, and oh-so-easy to shovel. "Morning."

The voice that escapes my throat is froggy, but all at once my body temperature is a degree hotter. Last night, after a quick game of chess, which I won, we hopped on the trolley and sang with the carolers, effectively taking out number eight on the Mission: Holly list.

Carm is going to kill me.

"Is that the list?" When I nod, he draws nearer. "I kinda hope I'm not working."

123

"What? How come?" The question takes precedence over the need to see if my name is listed. "This is only the biggest thing that's happened to Holly since the town was added to CNN's Best Cities to Live In list."

"It's going to be a mess. This place is going to be packed and for what? For a couple of middle-aged people to talk about their heyday? But"—his gaze moves from me to the list itself as he shrugs out of his coat—"I want the hours."

He goes on to tell me something about his schedule, but the words glide past me. All I notice is the heat from his body after he's finally out of his coat. It's like the siren call of warm sheets from the dryer—I want to snuggle into him.

Stoooop. I'm being paid to train him for one last day, and I can't allow him to ruffle my feathers, either from frustration or these ridiculous wayward thoughts, despite our truce.

"Lila?"

I shake myself from my trance.

Teddy eyes the list I'm still pointing to. The nail bed of my pointer finger is white because I'm pressing so hard. With a jolt, I keep on with the search. "Wait. There's a second page."

I flip the page up, but even before I can scan the paper, he says, "I'm in."

My heart leaps. Perhaps I'm on the list too. As my gaze nears the bottom, my hopes are dashed.

"Sorry, Santos." He smiles through gritted teeth. But, the fact that he cares takes the edge off the fact that he's once again taken my spot.

Again, it's not his fault.

"At least my mom has tickets already. It would have just been neat to work it." Then I read the rest of the page and gasp. "Holy crap, Teddy. Fifty percent sold out in five days!"

"Wow." Teddy stuffs his coat in the locker. "I don't know how Tita Lou does it."

"Because she's awesome."

"I guess so."

I frown. How could he not know that? But before I can ask, Ms. Velasco enters. "Hey, you two. Here's your task list for the day, if possible." She hands Teddy the list and waves goodbye, presumably to make her rounds to the Inn side.

Teddy reads off the list. "Hang icicle lights on windows. Remove shot glasses from display case, replace with snowflake ornaments. Remove blank journals and fill endcap with *Holiday by the Lake*. Easy-peasy."

We only have a four-hour shift. "Looks like we've got our work cut out for us today."

He looks down at me with a glint in his eyes, like I've issued a dare. "You think we can't get it done?"

I peer at him. "Is this motivation I detect? What have you done with the Teddy Rivera we know and don't love?"

He shuts the locker door and leans his shoulder against it. "Guess I had some fun last night, and I just thought . . ." He trails off.

"What?"

"Might as well try to take it easy on you for our last shift together."

"So you're going to say yes to whatever I ask you to do?" I cross my arms.

"Yeah. I will."

"All right, then." I brush past him and head toward the shop. From behind me he says, "I'm going to regret this, aren't I?"

An hour after opening the gift shop, I'm wiping down the doors of fingerprints when Teddy emerges from the hallway. He's carrying a box to the register labeled *Icicle lights.* He looks pained; I asked him to take on the lights, and I know his "suggestions" are ready to jump off his tongue.

It doesn't take long. "Here's what I think—"

I laugh. He's so predictable. "Nope. We'll outline the windows just like Ms. Velasco asked." I scrub the glass harder.

He grimaces. "Fine."

The windows on three of the four sides of the Bookworm Inn gift shop are floor to ceiling, with thick panes of glass. They're the second thing you see as you crest over the hill. The first, of course, is the turret of the main house, lit like a beacon every night. Add the lake behind it, which is a sparkling ribbon under the bright night sky and all together, it's a gorgeous sight.

When lights outline the windows, it takes the shop from impressive to spectacular. Because what warms the heart more than twinkle lights?

Whoever put the lights away last year, however, did not take their time. It was clearly the work of a seasonal part-timer who wasn't thinking about the people who would have to unravel them. I lift up the nest of wires and bulbs. This is going to take forever.

Teddy groans, and I can't even blame him.

Customers enter and head straight to our gift shop books area, to the biggest display: *The Holiday by the Lake* cookbook.

"I've got this." Teddy gestures to the box when a customer meanders close to the register.

"Sure?"

A grin lifts the right side of his face. "This isn't rocket science."

"I'm just saying." I hold both hands up with a laugh. "You're not exactly patient."

"Oh, I'm patient, Santos. I think you're confusing strategy with refusal."

"What do you need to strategize?"

"Everything's a puzzle. How many T-shirts we put up. How we get these lights on the window. Even where we set up the bobble-heads." He nods to the stack, now positioned in another part of the store. "Without strategy, you can be aimless."

"Like my rainbow shelves?" I gesture to the free library, which is now back in order.

"You don't think it did its job?"

I pause and consider. Since I put the books back in order, I *have* noticed fewer people milling around the gift shop. "I . . . guess it did."

"Aha! You liked it!"

"Maybe." I try to keep my smile contained, but it has a mind of its own. I might have made my point that it's sometimes better to do what's on the list, but every other time Teddy veered from it, something good emerged. The bobbleheads are now safely out of the way of traffic. Even my rainbow shelves, though technically incorrect for classification, was received well by library goers.

Is the predictable way the best way? Or is there room to be creative? Can I still be creative even with a bio major? What happens to my blog when my focus is on school?

My runaway thoughts have me on my feet. "I'll be back." I

smile at a group of women, clustered where the tree ornaments are displayed, grateful for the distraction. "Good morning! Welcome to the Bookworm Inn."

They're swift in their choices—they must be part of those tours that only allow a half hour at each stop—and approach the counter as a group. They coordinate with matching shirt colors, each with a travel cup of coffee in their hand (no wonder they're so chipper), wearing elf accessories. Their perfumes mix into what I imagine is a plume of smoke emanating above them. They all want a piece of the counter, like there are more secrets to the film behind the register.

The leader of the group, a Black woman wearing elf earrings, looks like she's about to burst. "So, we heard that Jonah Johanson is coming to the Inn. Is it true?"

"It is. Actually . . ." From under the counter, I retrieve a freshly printed flyer. Hands fly toward me like I'm a card dealer in Vegas.

"Oh my God," says a woman of Asian descent, with an elf hair clip holding back her silver-black hair, as she fans herself. "We have to find a way to come back!"

"Couldn't this have been scheduled at another time?" the shortest of the group, a fair-skinned blond woman, whines. "I still have family here for New Year's Eve."

The rest chime in with their opinions. One complains that she didn't have enough time to make plans; another says that she refuses to get out of her pj's until January second.

I can only stand there with a gritted smile. Because customers are always right, fangirls cannot be interrupted, and there's no one else in the gift shop for me to tend to.

At the window, Teddy's grinning, probably rolling in laughter in his head at my attempt to appease this tour group. He reaches up to hook the lights onto the Command strip I painstakingly hung last year. He'd taken off his green sweater, and is now in the Inn polo.

And his arms . . . they're on full display, and much closer than they were when he was climbing.

I mean, of course he's got arms, but apparently, what was hidden in his sweater were corded forearms and biceps and triceps. And hello, deltoids, and abs that peek out when he reaches up high. Even Carm wouldn't have failed this test.

Thank goodness for AP Bio.

"Do we need tickets?" The leader of the group waves the flyer. "Miss?"

"Um, what?" I say, tearing my eyes away.

"Tickets."

"Oh, yes. But we don't take payments here." I point to the flyer. "You'll have to go on the website or call this number."

"Have you read the book?" another person in the group asks. "I'm the only one who hasn't read the book or seen the movie. I'm just here for moral support." A sheepish smile appears on her face.

"Yes, I have. Though it's been years since I read the book. I actually saw the movie first." I cut short on telling the truth, that the book was just all right in comparison to the movie—which almost *never* happens, but this one's a rare exception. "In fact, we have copies around the corner. And the DVD and the CD soundtrack are over there."

That seems to satisfy the group—half of them scuttle back to pick up DVDs and CDs. Soon, their voices trail along with their footsteps as they leave the gift shop.

Which leaves me back to the quiet.

Then I hear a curse.

"Everything all right?" I no longer see Teddy. Glancing out the window, I see snowflakes flutter down like feathers after a pillow fight.

"I'm here, near the coffee cups."

Teddy is on his knees. He lifts a tangled mess of wires. "The second set of lights are being a pain. Can't seem to find where it goes haywire."

"Here, why don't I take one end and you take the other?" Dropping down on my knees, I plunge my fingers into the box and find the socket, then spread the lights between us.

We work on the strand of lights, him from his end and me from mine. It's silent except for our occasional grunts of frustration, admittedly more from me than from him. In fact, he's a little speed demon, his fingers working methodically through the strands.

My mind slides back to the training checklist. "Oh, I forgot to ask. Have you read the book?"

"Which one?"

"*Holiday by the Lake.*"

"Uh, no." He unravels another large knot.

"You've watched the movie, though?"

"Nope." He scoots on his knees closer to me so we're now a foot away.

I give him a horrified look. "It's part of the checklist! You need to know what this inn is about. Customers love to discuss the film."

"I know what the film's about, and what this business is about. It's a tourist trap, no disrespect to Tita Lou—but it's capitalizing on Hollywood and fame."

"I mean, that's true, but the way you say it sounds so harsh." I bite the side of my cheek.

"Why?"

"Because . . . besides this business being your aunt's, it's also the same business that hired me and that employs a good amount of the town. The people who come to visit the Inn also end up eating at Scrooge's, grabbing dessert at Blitzen's. They skate at the ice rink."

"I didn't think about it that way," he says, now only a knot away. His fingers stop, and he looks up at me. We're so close that when he speaks, it's a breath above a whisper. "Look, there's more to how I feel about this place. Tita Lou and my mom don't get along, and it's because of the Inn."

"I can't imagine anyone not getting along with Ms. Velasco."

He takes a breath. "When my Lola died, Tita chose to stay here even when she could have moved to California with my family. I respect her as a businesswoman and what she's done for this town, but from our point of view, she gave us up to be here. I'm here to work and climb for my competition, but that's all. My mom's not happy that I didn't come home, and I'm . . . I'm just trying to keep the peace."

"This explains—" I start.

"Explains what?"

"Your attitude. Of you acting like you both love and hate this place." Something my dad said earlier this week claws through. "But sometimes you need to make your own decisions. After all, you made the decision to stay here for Christmas. You all but threw yourself at your aunt. You could simply decide to want to be here. Look around. You're in the best place for Christmas."

His stare is serious, intent. "It's not that I don't want to be here."

"You don't?"

"No. Actually, this place is kind of growing on me." Teddy's face softens, like he's given up the fight. And maybe he's talking about more than just being in Holly.

The thought of it sends a tingle up my spine.

But the bell over the door rings.

Another customer.

TINSEL AND TROPES
A HOLIDAY BOOK BLOG

Title: The Dreidel Dilemma (Hanukkah Hijinks #2) by Liz Zimmerman
CATEGORY/GENRE: COZY MYSTERY

What compels you to keep a secret for someone else?

I couldn't stop thinking about book 1 (click here), so I splurged on an ebook for book 2, which was still an $11.99 purchase. I tried to keep that out of my mind while reading the book. (Here's a quick post on my expectations when I purchase ebooks above a certain threshold. Can you tell I'm still not over it?)

The Dreidel Dilemma takes secrets to another level. In this book, our protagonist from the first book is let in on a town's secret to keep a coveted and historical dreidel safe from a corrupt government organization that hired him in the first place. Several tropes come into play. Our protagonist must put up a front with his partner and act as if they're in a relationship, which ends in an office romance. All the while, he comes to terms with the importance of this dreidel to this community for the secret history it holds.

In the first book, *Menorah Mayhem*, we see that a secret can unite. In this book, the author asks: When are we culpable? If we enable the secret, then are we responsible for its consequences?

Was there enough Hanukkah in this book? Absolutely, and as much as I didn't want to read this because of its cliffhanger, knowing (through a quick Google search) that there are actually four books to this series, I wanted to see how the author would handle what felt like a more intricate plot against a Hanukkah backdrop.

And it was a good risk.

Pros: It's a book 2. I love sophomore books in a series—not a popular opinion, I know. In a usual three-book series, book 1 gives me the backstory and book 3 is the wrap-up, but book 2 is where I feel the characters come alive.

Cons: See above. Meaning that there's a little bit of a lull in this book. It's quieter, and it still ends in a frustrating cliffhanger.

Recommended for: Those who don't mind waiting for the big aha moment in a second book.

Rating: 4 stars

Chapter 14

Before I press publish on the post after work, I hesitate with my finger hovering over the mouse's button. It feels different now. This blog post is no longer being sent to my anonymous (tiny) mass of readers, or even to Carm. Now there's someone else, someone who's waiting for me to post, someone who knows me personally.

I'm doubting my words and my sentences. Was Teddy just placating me when he said I was a good writer? How many of my posts has he read?

I shake my head, the angel taking root on my shoulder, knocking the devil off. TnT is my passion. The blog has been around longer than I've known Teddy, and will be around after he leaves.

I press down on the button decisively just as my door slams open.

"I'm ready to shop," Irene demands, and lifts a torn piece of notebook paper. "I've got a list."

"Why did you wait until the last minute—" I shut my laptop and do a double take. Irene has on an over-the-shoulder teal sweatshirt, frayed around the neckline. But one fact keeps me from telling her that she looks utterly cute today. "Is that my shirt?"

"What, this old thing? It was in my closet."

"It was probably in your closet because you put it there."

"It would help if you actually did your laundry so that you could fold it and put it into your own closet."

"Are you stalking my dirty laundry?"

"Nope." She spins and heads down the hallway, her ponytail swinging from side to side. "I'm stalking your clean laundry."

I growl under my breath but scan my room. It *is* a mess today. Clothes are strewn every which way. A stack of mail—solicitations from colleges, some in thick envelopes—wait for me on my bed-side dresser.

All evidence that I haven't had much free time. I had my shift this morning with Teddy, and this afternoon I'm doing some last-minute Christmas shopping with Irene. Tonight is a Mission: Holly night with Carm and KC.

I don't work on Christmas Eve or Christmas day, and now that I no longer have training shifts with Teddy, my workdays are as sparse as the bare tree limbs of the oak tree outside my window.

A notification beeps in—it's a comment on my blog. Santa with a View again: *Secrets aren't such a bad thing.*

It's followed by a link to the BookGalley internship.

My heart speeds up. Who is this person?

Another notification, this time a text from Teddy.

Teddy: *Nice post*

Lila: Are you trolling me?

135

Teddy: I don't even like to read blogs.

This isn't true. He picked his last book through a blogger recommendation.

Lila: Right . . .

Teddy: Bloggers tend to navel gaze.

Lila: Sort of like how climbers are only worried about their climb.

Teddy: There's nowhere to go but up.

Lila: So that makes you . . . ?

Teddy: Focused. Determined.

Lila: Self-centered.

Teddy: Ha. And bloggers are?

I think about it.

Lila: Thoughtful, introspective.

Teddy: Equally self-centered.

Lila: Blogs are supposed to be self-centered. They're my words.

> **Teddy:** Just like climbers are supposed to be focused on their own climb

I growl, and yet, under all that, my body hums from the energy of our text banter. Is it silly to admit that I'm going to miss our in real-life banter now that we're no longer working together?

> **Teddy:** Anyway, that's not why I'm texting.

> **Lila:** ?

> **Teddy:** Can you cover my shift tonight? I need to climb

I laugh. Still, I'm grateful, even if I already have plans.

> **Lila:** I'm busy tonight
> Sledding at Wonderhill, and we already bought tickets

"Ate!" Irene yells now, at the top of her lungs. "Please!"

I grab my wallet from my desk and stuff my phone in my back pocket.

As I slip into the driver's seat of my car, Irene's lips curl into a grin. "What's up with you?"

"What?" Breathless from the cold, I blow into my gloved hands and then turn on the ignition.

"You're so happy."

My eyes dart upward to the rearview mirror. Sure enough, I have a grin on my face.

Teddy: *So when you blog a review, how do you decide when something is a half-star? Stars don't exist in halves, do they?*

I'm staring at Teddy's next jab. We have been sparring over text for the last three hours, all through Christmas shopping. I've just walked into the house, Irene at my heels with bags of presents. Pulling off my beanie, I scatter beads of water on the floor. "We're home!" I scream down the hallway at the twins and my mother, wherever they are. Then I lob my next text comment.

> **Lila:** How bored are you that you're thinking about my blogging instead of your climbing?

> **Teddy:** Actually climbing > blogging

> **Lila:** Intellect > Brawn

"Ate! Help?"

I look behind me—Irene's stuck in the doorway. I'd shut the door on her, so engrossed in my texts. I double back to open it. With her puffy jacket, hat pulled over her eyes, and two bags in each hand, she could pass for a taller Randy, Ralphie's little brother in *A Christmas Story.*

Once she's inside, I inch up her beanie to expose her eyeballs.

"Thanks a lot." She's glaring at me as if I haven't given her the time of her life. I was pretty much a cabdriver with all the stores I took her to. It's actually quite impressive that she saved enough money to buy presents.

Resourceful, that one.

"You've been glued to your phone all afternoon." She hefts the bags onto the kitchen table, grunting.

It's no use pretending I haven't been. "It's work."

My phone beeps, and my heart leaps. What *is* up with me? Am I in such need of company and friends that I look forward to verbally sparring (either in text or in real life) with my ex-nemesis? But I grab my phone anyway and read the text. Still Teddy.

> **Teddy:** So if you had a recommendation for the first holiday book to pick up, what would it be?

I snigger. Yeah, right, he's interested.

> **Lila:** Quit teasing

> **Teddy:** No. I swear.

"Work. Suuure, Ate." Irene shrugs out of her outer layers and lets them all drop on the floor. It's my absolute biggest pet peeve. Because who ends up picking up after her? Me.

"You can't just leave your stuff here, Irene."

Mom walks in—she's already in her scrubs, and she's fiddling with one of her teddy bear earrings. "Hi, girls." She kisses Irene on the forehead—my little sister scuttles away, of course—and does the same to me.

I glance at the clock. "It's only five."

"Honey, I'm going in a little early. The evening shift's short-staffed. Can you take the twins to a birthday party?"

"I have sledding with Carm. What time?"

Mom pulls a frown. "Six-thirty. I already RSVP'd and they

will be so disappointed if they can't go. And Dad's working late since it's crunch time at the shop. I would want you to stay at the party too. You know how rowdy your brothers get sometimes."

"Um . . . okay," I say as I scoop up our clutter so Mom can maneuver her way through the kitchen. There's no real choice here. With both parents working, I have to step up.

But Carm's not going to like it. Our tickets are for 8:30 p.m. I send a new text message:

> **Lila:** Gotta play big sis tonight and take twins to a birthday party. I can meet you at WH? Party is at 630, so I should still be able to make it after.

> **Carm:** :(
> Can you really make it?

I put my backward planning to work, and wince.

> **Lila:** It will be tight, but I think I can.

While I wait for a response—and the mere fact that the text bubbles haven't appeared means that Carm is ticked—I ask, "Where's the party at, Mom?"

"Oh geez, honestly I'm not sure." Mom fills up tiny plastic containers with leftover food for her lunch break, which loosely means at about two in the morning. "Something about a climbing gym?"

"Climb Holly?" My heart thrums.

"Yep, that's it."

And as if I manifest him, a text buzzes in from Teddy:

No recommendation from a book blogger? You're not doing your job.

Lila: Don't you have work to do?

Teddy: Work? What's work?

Dots show on his side of the screen.

Teddy: Actually yes, I'm working. I'll be here awhile.

Which means he won't be at Climb Holly when I'm there for the party.

"Lila?" Mom is at the door, jacket on, with her purse and lunch bag at the ready. "Everything good?"

"Yep. Taken care of."

But a small part of me is disappointed that Teddy won't be there.

Chapter 15

An hour and twenty-five minutes later, in Climb Holly's parking lot, Grant yells from the backseat, "Hurry, hurry, Ate Lila. We're going to be late!"

"We should have left earlier," Graham fusses. "They probably already have their gear on. We're never going to get to climb."

"Shhh. I can't focus." I scan the parking lot for an empty space. It is a jungle of vehicles, of cars trailing after pedestrians to grab their spots. While there are more spaces down the long road to the gym, the packed snow is a bear to trudge through.

"There's one!" Graham yells. His arm is like an arrow that appears next to my head. I swivel my car into the space, but there's a compact car in the tiny slot.

"Sh—" I begin, but press my lips together. The last thing I need is for one of my brothers to let it slip that I cursed.

We left much later than expected. I started on a Christmas romance that I couldn't set down and lost track of time. Now there's no easy parking.

"How many people did your friend invite?" I grumble.

"The whole class," they say in unison.

"Geez." I round the parking lot once more. "It's not looking good, guys. We might have to park a little farther down."

"That's okay, we have boots!"

My seat jolts forward as Grant stomps against the back of my chair.

In the distance, the taillights of a car flash. I speed up just in time; another car had rolled into the parking lot. With my brothers cheering in my ear, I slide into the space.

As we climb out of the car and I sling my backpack onto my shoulder, I say, "Hey, listen up. There are rules."

Both grumble, but I ignore it. The first thing one learns in babysitting is that rules and boundaries must be clear. And unlike a certain person I know, I actually believe that rules create a more ordered life.

Quit thinking about him.

And yet, I do, especially now that I'm back on his turf.

"I'm going to try and find a table inside to do my homework." I cringe at the lie. What I plan to do is write a draft of my next blog post, since I'm just a few chapters away from finishing this Christmas romance.

"Homework? But there's no school until January!" Graham says.

"Yes, but I'd rather get it done so I don't have to think about it. Don't you want to go into Christmas and the New Year knowing that your schedule is clear?"

"No. I just forget about it." Grant stomps ahead.

Graham throws open the metal door and a roar of noise greets us, interspersed with the occasional shriek. A group of elementary schoolers huddle near the entrance, and by the way my brothers throw themselves in the middle of the group, this must be their class.

I spot a mom with a pointed party hat, chatting up other parents and thumbing her phone. Standard pre-party chat. That must be Mrs. Pruitt, the birthday boy's mother.

I wait my turn as, one by one, the parents walk past, leaving me as the last (technical) adult with the kids, who have started to crash into one another like the beginnings of a mosh pit.

"Hi. I'm Grant and Graham's sister." I point them out. "My mom already signed the waiver, and it should be in the gym's system."

"Okay . . . okay," Mrs. Pruitt says through gritted teeth. The kids have shed their jackets, and they are swinging them around like nunchucks.

"Um . . ." I hesitate. I've got things to do, but my brothers are in the middle of this faux martial arts performance. So I rush toward them and lay a hand on each of my brother's shoulders. At the contact, their faces turn up at me.

Being an *ate* is a big deal. While my friends might not have any real idea what that means, in my family, when my parents aren't around, I'm in charge. My dad still calls his big sister *Ate*. And as much as my little brothers have attitude and mess around, when I pull rank, they fall behind like soldiers.

My hands on them mean they should seriously chill out. Which they do.

Just in time, a Climb Holly employee in the company's yellow polo—and now I'm really, really glad for the Bookworm Inn's forest green because, wow, yellow is loud—shows up in the middle of the group. The kids turn to her like she's Santa himself.

"Hi, everyone. Welcome. My name is Sarah and I'm going to be your party planner today."

I backpedal gingerly, like I'm in the middle of a heist. Two more steps and I'll be scot-free. Worst-case scenario, if there isn't a quiet spot inside the gym, I'll hide out in my car until the party's over.

When I spin on my heel, I collide with Mrs. Pruitt. Half of her lipstick has been licked dry; she's frazzled. And her eyes . . .

"Can you stay?" she says.

"Oh, I'm sorry. I—"

"Please? I bit off more than I can chew. You have a big family. You know how to take care of kids. And you babysit, right?"

"I do. But—"

"Honestly, I didn't think so many folks would RSVP since it's so close to Christmas. But they all did. Said yes, I mean." Her eyes dart at the loud roar of cheers from the kids.

Sarah raises a hand to the group. "All right. Let's head on to the locker area and we'll store your coats."

"You have a party planner," I remind Mrs. Pruitt.

"She can only do so much. There's sure to be a rogue kid or two. Please. I'll pay you. Well."

Mrs. Pruitt divulges her rate. It's beyond what I consider fair. But more than that, her face has skewed to the point of desperation.

The sound of my brothers yelping is the thing that breaks my hesitation. If these other kids are all as rambunctious as them, then Mrs. Pruitt and Sarah combined will still be outnumbered.

"Yes, okay," I concede.

"Great. I'll sign you in. You'll need to do a waiver too."

I heave a breath and follow the group to the locker room.

Jumping in right away, I help direct traffic, dole out shoes—who knew they had to rent shoes!—and pile jackets in one area. Then I bring all the gifts to the party room, where the cake is already set up in the middle with balloons around it.

I sign my waiver on the go. Afterward, I help usher the kids to the big rock wall, where there's a person standing with their back to us. Now I get why they wear yellow—we can see this person from far away, and they stand out from the other climbers. Next to them is a pile of rope.

"I'd like to introduce you to my assistant," Sarah says.

The kids all but rush toward the instructor standing on the elevated thick pad that covers the entire bottom of the area under the wall. Mrs. Pruitt and I trail behind as the assistant turns around.

It's Teddy.

What's he doing here? He's supposed to be at the Inn.

It makes no sense why I'm nervous, but my first instinct is to hide behind Mrs. Pruitt. Except, she's shorter than me. So I turn my body toward the exit I should have used ten minutes ago.

In my periphery, Sarah takes her place next to Teddy. "All right, everyone. Let's go over some rules. Now, I know rules don't sound like fun but it's important to keep everyone safe. Everyone must follow them. Got it?" After a collective agreement that rumbles through the group, she says, "Now everyone take a seat."

Sarah continues. "Go ahead and sit cross-legged. This little briefing is going to take a few minutes. In total, we're going to be spending three hours together with my assistant Teddy."

Three hours? Crap. My Wonderhill plans are crumbling.

As Sarah continues to speak, I text Carm, who'd sent a simple *ok* after my last text. I wince as I type:

> **Lila:** I don't know if I can make it after all
>
> This thing is 3 hours long
>
> I'm sorry

> **Carm:** I guess I'll just reschedule

> **Lila:** I owe you

". . . We're going to have two lanes, where I will be on belay as well as Teddy." Sarah continues as I tuck my phone back into my pocket. I'm saddled with guilt. How am I going to make it up to Carm?

"Being on belay means that I am on this side of the rope so you can safely climb. But in order for us to properly show you how to climb, I'm going to have Teddy demonstrate with another person. The first task is getting you into the harness. Can we have a volunteer?" Sarah laughs as hands shoot up. "I'm so impressed with your enthusiasm, but I didn't finish my sentence. I'd love to have one of the adults come up and participate."

"How about one of you back there?" Teddy says, interrupting my thoughts.

I feel like I'm at war with myself. The confident side of me doesn't give a crap that he's here. The shy side wants to crawl under the soft mats that line the floors.

How did I not notice that he had a nice voice?

"She can do it," Mrs. Pruitt says, turning to me with a hopeful smile.

I blink back at her.

"Oh." Teddy lifts a hand over his eyes, lips curling into a grin. "Oh, hello there. I know you."

Girding myself unsuccessfully, I walk forward. *Let's just get this over with.*

"You know my sister?" Graham calls out.

"I do. We work together at the Bookworm Inn. She trained me." Then he adds, "But now it's my turn to show you a thing or two."

My face erupts into flames.

"Everyone, pay attention," Teddy says. "I'm going to assist Lila into a harness. We'll do this a step at a time with each of you, but I want you to know what to expect. So eyes up here, please."

Twenty pairs of eyes lock on him.

Impressive. Where is this Teddy at the Bookworm Inn? In spite of my hesitance to help with this demonstration, I want to see more of this.

"This is a harness." He raises the contraption and goes through its parts. But my focus shifts to the foreboding wall behind Teddy. Looking up, I trace the different-colored markers all the way up to the ceiling, to a pulley system and a bell.

"Now Lila is going to step into it."

The sentence snaps me back to the present. "What?"

He shakes the harness in encouragement.

"Oh . . . oh no." I realize this was the basis of my volunteering, but suddenly I want to be anywhere but here.

A chant begins from the audience, at first quiet. I hear my

brothers' voices rising above the rest. Seconds later, I make out the words.

"Step in it. Step in it. Step in it."

I've stepped in it, all right. I roll my eyes, though inside the peer pressure is real. I always do what's expected.

The volume turns up from a three to an eight.

"Okay, fine." I relent, because I don't want to look like I'm scared, nor do I want to disappoint.

My decision sets off applause from the audience, and Teddy's face brightens. He holds out the harness. The two holes for my legs are obvious, and I step in while he keeps hold. Still, I have to bend down as it snags on my joggers and have no choice but to lay both hands on his shoulders to keep steady.

"Easy does it," he whispers.

This close, I can smell the hint of bar soap and mint. It's pleasant in comparison to the rest of this gym.

"Now you'll see that Teddy is pulling up the harness so that it's at her waist," Sarah says.

His fingers slide around the harness so it's at my hip, his knuckle grazing against me.

I hold my breath to keep my heart from leaping out of my throat.

He gently turns me around so the buckle at my waist is visible to the group. "Then I'm going to make sure that this part is nice and secure."

He really does have a nice voice, and all at once my heart retreats into my chest cavity and thumps a million times an hour. The way he moves his hands around me, at the buckle at my waist, to the ones at my legs to make sure I don't fall out in the hypothetical event I flip upside down, though still respectful, has the same effect on me as the Christmas romance I just read.

"Now I'm going to hook you onto the rope."

And then those warm feelings hurtle to the ground. "No. No way."

Understanding flits across his face. "You don't have to go up the wall," he says softly. "I'll just hook you up. Is that okay?"

His expression is sincere, and when I look into his eyes, I find no hint of malintent. I believe him. It takes a beat for me to find my voice. "Okay."

He walks me away from the group, and we stand next to the wall. He pulls a rope with a carabiner at the end. "This carabiner? It will be attached to the carabiner on your harness, but I'm attached to it too. I am what you call the belay. I'll make sure you're absolutely safe."

"The carabiners on your key ring." It's the only thing I can think to say. "It makes sense."

"It's always handy to have one around. But also it's a reminder." His voice is steady, soothing.

"Of what?"

"What I love to do. It keeps me focused."

Right then, Teddy has all my focus.

"I thought you were working tonight?"

"This is work, sort of." A small smile graces his lips. "Truth now. You okay?"

"Yes. No. Not really."

"It's all right. You can trust me. You're not going up unless you say you want to."

His words are surprisingly comforting. I take a deep breath.

The click of the carabiners startles me, and my gaze drops to my waist, where his hands are on the link.

"It's as easy as that, folks," he says, facing the crowd. "Then all you have to do is climb. I'll be your belay on one of the ropes, and Sarah will be on the other. Whenever you're done, all you have to do is say you're ready to come down. Then you can simply do so, or let go and we'll ease you from the wall."

I reach up to touch one of the holds and shake it. Sure enough, it's secure and solid. The red ones are especially prominent, sticking out at least a couple of inches. From here, it doesn't look that bad. And yet, it's not the going up that scares me, but the coming down. It's the misstep, the feeling of not being able to catch myself.

"All right, you're done. Thank you for helping to demonstrate," Teddy says to me as Sarah lines the children up. "You did well."

"I guess," I say. "Should I take all this off?" I start to fuss with the carabiner, just as he reaches out, and our hands collide. I bite my lip from the rush of giddiness that mixes with my uncertainty.

"Sorry." He clears his throat, eyes rising briefly to my face. His expression is different from the other looks he's given me, and his cheeks pink before he looks away. He unhooks the carabiner and works quickly at loosening the buckles, though he's gentle and professional. He's so at ease being this close to me. He's probably so at ease being this close to anyone if he's helping them with their harnesses.

To move the moment forward, I force small talk. "How often do you work events like this?"

"Not often, but I was here for practice, and I got someone to take my shift at the gift shop. I get a little bit of a discount when I help out with these big groups. Tita Lou doesn't know about this either."

"God, so many secrets."

"Like someone I know." His eyebrows lift.

"I won't tell her, I promise," I say, just to make it clear. Because I'm involved now too.

It reminds me of my blog post from the other day. What exactly are we enabling with each other, and is it a good thing?

TINSEL AND TROPES
A HOLIDAY BOOK BLOG

Title: There's No Place Like Home During Christmas by Wanda Strong
GENRE: ADULT CONTEMPORARY ROMANCE

Do opposites really attract?

The setup of this book was pure perfection. The setting was gorgeous. Both protagonists were likable and in general, kind. And the plot, about a real estate agent and the town mayor who've hated each other's guts since they both competed throughout high school but must band together to help the town B&B, is cute enough. Though yes, the representation has much to be desired—in the large cast of characters, there were only two people of color. I mean, I've lived in a small town all my life and, trust me, we exist. (Yes,

I'm probably starting to sound like a broken record, but here's <u>my post</u> about the lack of diversity in books, especially in small town romances.)

But of all the romance tropes, the enemies-to-lovers arrangement is the hardest for me to get on board with. After the couple gets stuck during a snowstorm—hello, forced proximity!—suddenly the same things that used to annoy them are now endearing?

How does that even work in real life? Can you ever really forget someone else's faults? Physical attraction only goes so far, doesn't it?

And yet, this book worked for me. It really did. It was the "only one bed" trope that sealed the deal. And sometimes you just need a happy ending. I also think the little bit of magic that played out in the book helped too. Sorry, I'm not spoiling!

Pros: Perfect reading when it's cold outside.

Cons: I think I want more heat next time.

Recommended for: Those looking for a new book boyfriend, because the hero is swoonworthy.

Rating: 4 stars

Chapter 16

The six of us burst into the house. It's negative one million degrees outside, and the twins are cranky. Snow spills onto the linoleum floor as each of us sheds our coat and boots, shivering as we enter the kitchen.

"I'm so hungry!" Graham says.

"When can we open presents?" Grant asks.

"After noche buena." Mom is already in the kitchen, taking food out of the oven, which was kept on warm while we were at children's Mass.

We start setting the table, grabbing the special tableware from the buffet. It's like an assembly line with the twins putting down the placemats and napkins, Irene with the utensils, and me with the plates and bowls, while Mom's Christmas playlist filters in from the background.

Jingling comes from the tree, and tinsel flutters to the ground. Dad emerges from the back, glitter dotting his forehead. A present is in his hand, and he slips it between the pine branches.

I look down and bite my lip. It's his present to Mom.

"Bringing the food to the table," Mom warns.

The kids rush to sit, and Dad and I help Mom bring the food over: A large soup tureen filled with arroz caldo, a plate of liempo, and leche flan. It's a small menu since it's just us, but it's special and filling so we can fall asleep straight after we open our family presents.

We are virtually silent except for the occasional moan—the food is that good. It takes a mere fifteen minutes before the twins wiggle in their chairs with their bowls licked clean. Still, they hold their tongues, knowing what I learned pretty quickly at their age: The less they distract, the faster the parents finish eating and the quicker we get to open presents.

Mom is in the middle of scooping more arroz caldo into her bowl when she says, without looking up, "Want to open presents?"

"Really?" Irene's face lights up. "But you're not done."

"You all are being so patient." Mom laughs and nods toward the living room. "Why not switch it up this year?"

The whole table cheers, and even Dad leaps from the table. Mom follows us to the family room with her bowl and takes a corner of the couch. Irene and the twins sit cross-legged next to the tree, as do I.

It doesn't matter that I'm eighteen. Right now, I might as well be the twins' age.

"You all know the rule," Mom explains, as she does every year. Tomorrow morning, we'll get Santa presents, presents from other families, and the kid presents to one another—or, my and Irene's presents to everyone else—but these Christmas Eve presents are from Mom and Dad. It keeps it special, keeps it about us.

Each one of us is given a package. One I know about, because we get this every year. We all dig into the wrapper with gusto, and wrapping paper flies everywhere.

"This is exactly what I wanted!" Next to me, Irene shrieks and lifts up pajamas printed with bacon and eggs all over.

We're talking all at once. Graham's pj's feature dogs of all breeds. Grant's have army men. Dad has spectacles printed on his, and Mom's has nurse's hats—which she picked out.

These yearly pajamas are a mainstay. And each year, Mom outdoes herself.

These pajamas are footed.

"Your turn, Ate!" Graham yells from the hallway. He's halfway undressed and peeking around the corner.

"Patience!" I laugh. Under the tissue paper is fuzzy fabric, and when I lift it out of the box, I notice the print.

They're stethoscopes.

"It's perfect!" Dad says. "For our future doctor."

Future doctor.

It's a statement I've made time and again. I even said it earlier this week, to Teddy, when he asked me what I wanted to major in.

But now, for some reason, it feels like a true commitment. Even more than it was to declare it on my applications as my intended major.

"Put them on, Ate," Irene says, already in her pajamas.

"Oh, okay," I say, snapping out of it. *You're being dramatic.* I hustle to my bedroom to change. The fabric is ultrasoft. Looking in the mirror, I see an overgrown toddler reflected back. Except I'm not. I'm an eighteen-year-old wearing footed pajamas. An eighteen-year-old with a secret I have yet to divulge. And why haven't I done so?

All this time, my blog, my writing identity, was just a hobby, something separate. But is it more? And what do I do with it?

My phone buzzes on my desk, interrupting my thoughts. It's a requirement to leave it at home for Mass, so I check my notifications. There are lots from the blog, some texts, and one message from Teddy.

After seeing him at the climbing gym yesterday, I haven't been able to get him out of my mind, nor could I erase the memories of him standing so close.

Teddy: So I guess I'm coming over for dinner?

Startled, I text immediately.

Lila: When?

Teddy: Day after Christmas
Your parents didn't say?

No, they hadn't. Ms. Velasco always comes to our Leftover Christmas party every year on the twenty-sixth. It's when everyone brings a repurposed leftover to help ease their refrigerator.

But it didn't dawn on me that Teddy would be coming over too.

"Mom?" I set the phone facedown and rush downstairs. The family is seated in front of the fire, five out of five in their footed pajamas.

"We've been waiting for you. Do you like the pajamas?" Mom says.

Oh, duh. We were still in the middle of presents. "Yes, I'm sorry. I . . . The zipper got stuck. I love it. Thank you." I bend down to kiss each of my parents on the cheek. I'll ask them about the party later.

"Before you all open the rest of our presents . . ." Dad stands, and despite looking very silly in his footed pajamas, his face is serious. He sticks his hand in the tree and pulls out the box.

My eyes dart between him and Mom. "For me?" she says, as if he doesn't give her a present every year.

He nods.

She opens Dad's present, and her face beams when she sees it. "Arturo." She lifts up the mother's bracelet, four strands of our birthstones strung into one. "You didn't stick to the budget we discussed. This is not twenty-five dollars!"

He wraps it around her wrist and gently clasps the ends together. "Sometimes rules are meant to be broken."

"I love it." Mom throws her arms around Dad's neck.

For a moment, they seem to melt into one another. Irene leans toward me and snuggles into my arm, and with that, all my worries are washed away. This is what Christmas is all about. Even when we didn't have any money for gifts, we never lost this. At our lowest point, who we are as a family remained. The important things don't change.

"Now it's the kids' turn." Dad pulls gifts from behind the tree. One by one, he hands us a package. Mine is a solid, heavy box.

The mood ramps up, and the four of us dig into the wrapping paper. My siblings squeal. Everyone is yelling, but I can't tear my eyes away from what's in front of me.

It's a brand-new laptop. "Oh my God."

"You've been working with the same laptop for a while, and

since you share yours with Irene most days, we thought it was time for a new one to bring to school," Mom says.

"This is . . . wow." I was fully resigned to use my laptop until it died or all the keys fell off. I know how much this costs. I can probably tell you how many hours it would take for me to earn enough to buy this laptop. "Are you sure?"

"What do you mean, are we sure?" Dad glances at Mom for a beat, then says, "We want you to have everything you need to succeed."

Inside me is a balloon that's been inflated, filled with gratitude and joy. But it's also taut with uncertainty and guilt. My parents have sacrificed and worked hard to get back on their feet. For me to succeed.

But what does that really mean?

Christmas Day passes like a vivid dream, from the twins' early wakeup just shy of 5:00 a.m. so that we can open gifts, through brunch and early dinner, which consists of the usual suspects: lumpia and pancit, fried chicken and ham, bibingka, and Filipino fruit salad. The house is turned upside down, the noise level rises and falls depending on who's in charge of the playlist, and the fire is kept lit throughout the day.

It is glorious. And like every year, even those lean years, I am swept up in all of it. There's no rush, no pressure to be anywhere. There is just relaxing, and lounging, and something I never do during the rest of the year: Napping.

I'm still in my footed pajamas, though I did wash my face and brush my teeth this morning, and I pulled my Ate card and demanded the chaise part of our L-shaped couch. I lie down on my side and watch Grant, who is playing with his army men on the ottoman in front of the fireplace. Without Graham, he's much calmer, and watching him set up the little figures is like ASMR for the eyes.

I was just as methodical with my Legos when I was a kid. I imagined worlds and built them one brick at a time. Yes, I would build them according to the box's instructions, but shortly after, I'd take it all apart and rebuild it anew. Sometimes I took parts from other sets to put together one new world.

That's how I built my high school life. One class, one club, one interest, until something bigger materialized. But while it's so easy to change your mind with Legos if you don't like the structure, what happens if you simply want to change your mind about the future? At what point can I switch things up? Is there even such a thing?

My phone buzzes next to my face.

Teddy: *Merry Christmas*

I blink with heavy eyelids.

> **Lila:** Merry Christmas

> **Teddy:** I hate to say it but I miss you

I gasp, now wide awake.

> **Teddy:** There's no one nagging me about anything

I laugh, and Grant turns to me with a goofy grin. He's holding up a figurine. Then I have an idea. "Grant, smile," I prompt.

His smile grows wider, spanning from ear to ear. I snap a picture and send it to Teddy. This, I realize, is the first photo I've texted him, and my mind races. Was that a good move? Our conversations are always laced with a little sarcasm and right now, there's no hint of it.

I'm confused about lots of things these days.

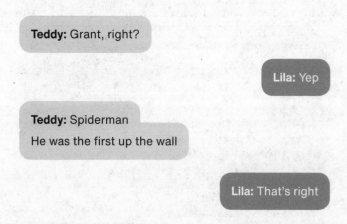

Teddy: Grant, right?

Lila: Yep

Teddy: Spiderman
He was the first up the wall

Lila: That's right

At the birthday party, Teddy called Grant *Spider-Man*.

My phone buzzes with another text. It's a picture of Teddy holding up a Spider-Man graphic novel.

A. Graphic. Novel. My heart flutters.

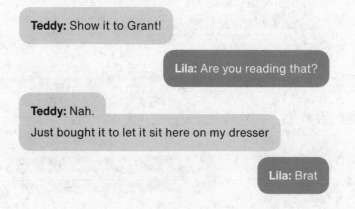

Teddy: Show it to Grant!

Lila: Are you reading that?

Teddy: Nah.
Just bought it to let it sit here on my dresser

Lila: Brat

"Grant." I wave my brother over and show him the screen. "Look."

"Whoa, that's cool!" Grant gives me a thumbs-up. I take another pic of him and send it.

> **Teddy**: My man!

Warmth fills my chest. I settle back into the chaise, texting on my side.

> **Lila**: I have a sister too
> Irene
> **Lila**: A freshman

> **Teddy**: Three years apart
> Like my mom and Tita Lou
> Do you both get along?

> **Lila**: We're sisters
> It's complicated

> **Teddy**: I hear you
> I feel the complication
> Not sure how to handle the complication
> I run from complication

> **Lila**: Climb you mean?

> **Teddy**: Touché

> **Lila**: Your Tita Lou is pretty great

A text doesn't follow; Teddy either got sidetracked or he doesn't want to talk about it anymore. Which I understand completely. If the Velascos and Riveras are anything like my family, the need for privacy is paramount.

I heft myself off the couch and find myself alone. Grant must have wandered off in the middle of me texting, and the house is unusually silent. I make sure that the fireplace door is shut, grab a cup of apple cider, and then, as I've been taught by babysitting, wander through the house to locate all of my people.

Wouldn't you know, everyone is in their bedrooms. Except for Irene. She's on my bed, half asleep.

The first thing that comes to my mind: write a blog post.

The second thing: I have a new computer.

It's still under the tree, so I grab it and open the box. I run my hand over the unmarred, sleek and silver top and open it to a pristine keyboard. And when I press the on button, it wakes with a soothing chime.

The rest of the installation and updates happen in a breeze. After, I log on to the dashboard of my blog. More comments await my reply, the newest submitted once again from Santa with a View, sent just ten minutes ago.

Again, it's a link to the BookGalley internship.

"What a nag." Still, I click on the link, which leads me to the page once more. This time, I settle in and read through the qualifications: at least eighteen years old, good organizational skills, interest in books, avid reader, can work with documents and spreadsheets. It's followed by a simple form, which acts as a cover letter, and a prompt for a five-hundred-word essay, much like the college essays I filled out in the last five months. Finally, there's an upload button for a résumé or a CV, which I have worked on as part of college prep class last semester. The deadline to submit the application is the twenty-sixth. Tomorrow.

I am definitely qualified. Especially if I link to my blog as part of my résumé.

What does it say about who I want to be if I apply? Science versus the arts. Medicine versus writing. While applying isn't the nail in the coffin, by doing this, I'm pulling all the plywood out. I'm getting the hammer ready.

It's tempting.

Suddenly, the house seems to wake, with one of the twins complaining that they're hungry.

It's the push I need, and the pressure jolts my body forward. With swift fingers, I type in my contact info and cut and paste one document into another. I upload my photo and CV and heave a breath. I'm about to match my name with my blog. There's no turning back. After I make this connection, I will no longer be anonymous.

Usually, I only make decisions after tons of research. I consult with others. I take my time. But somehow with encouragement from Carm, Teddy, and even this anonymous Santa with a View, it's enough.

I shut my eyes and press send.

My phone beeps with an email confirmation that my résumé has been sent. All at once my heart rate doubles.

Holy crap, I did it.

I did it.

Chapter 17

Teddy: What are you wearing?

Lila: ?
Clothes?

Teddy: Yeah, thanks smartie. For real

Lila: Like right now?

Teddy: No. For dinner tonight

Lila: I'm not thinking that far ahead
I'm helping my mom cook

Mom shoves a spoonful of stuffing into my mouth, successfully distracting me from Teddy's texts. "Taste this." The stuffing is just shy of piping hot, and I chew while sipping air. Still, the flavors pop. Apples and leftover cubes of liempo and onion, mixed in with toasted day-old homemade bread. "Well?"

"It's perfect."

"You think?"

"I don't think. I know."

"All right, time to put it in the warmer." Mom sticks the entire stainless-steel pan into the oven, where a ham pot pie and stir-fry green beans already reside. On the stove is a small pot of gravy, just finished, with mashed potatoes. Cooling under tin foil is embutido made with leftover shredded chicken. She eyes her watch. "And right on time for my shower. Can you handle the kitchen until guests arrive?"

I raise an eyebrow. "How many parties have I helped you pull off?"

"You're right." She cups my face with both her hands and kisses me on the forehead. "I don't know what I'll do when you leave for college. Who's going to help me keep this place a little less chaotic?"

Except for the dishes piled up in the sink (the dishwasher is already running), the house is party ready. I took my turn in the shower this morning, so all I have to do is jump into fresh clothes when Mom's all done.

If Teddy thinks Ms. Velasco is too precise with her opening and closing checklists, he's going to have another thing coming when he meets my mother, who has every event planned to a T.

At the thought of Teddy, my cheeks flush. Our texts have been nonstop. But now he's coming to my house. My. House. "Did anyone cancel?" I ask, wincing on the inside. In truth, I both hope and don't hope that he decides to come. Texts and photos are one thing, but in person . . .

"Still expecting five people. Lou and Teddy, Carm, Frank, and Trish. Super easy guest list." She unties her apron. "Have you worked with Teddy since you've trained him? Is everything better?"

"What do you mean better?"

"Irene told me that he was giving you some problems."

Of course. I roll my eyes. "She's such a snoop. How does she even know?"

"Your siblings are very observant, and anyway it shouldn't be something you keep from me. I want to be able to support you if you're struggling."

Guilt slashes through me about my sent application.

I focus on the topic at hand. "It's fine, Mom. He and I are . . . good." Though, as I say it, I consider what our status is. Are we friends? Just coworkers who exchange dozens of messages per day? Conspirators from our shared secrets?

She hangs her apron on the hook next to the pantry door. "I met him once before, you know."

"You have?" I turn and grab for anything to use as a tool for . . . something. Snapping a paper towel from the roll, I pretend-wipe up the imaginary spills on the stove.

"When he was a little boy. You were probably twelve? He just turned thirteen. His parents were visiting New York City, and they passed through town to visit Lou. Though that was the last time they visited."

"What's up with them anyway?" I ask casually.

"The relationship is quite contentious. It's sad, really. And it always makes me think of you and Irene. I want the two of you to be close, through the ups and downs. Family is all we have."

"I know, Mom."

"Anyway, he was such a sweet kid back then. Very curious, but shy. But now he has earrings."

Oh dear, here we go. My parents, in addition to their privacy standards, have somewhat superficial standards when it comes to "proper" grooming and attire. It's old-fashioned and tiring. I snort. "Is that what's bothering you?"

"No, of course not. And I'm not bothered." She sighs. "What can I say, I'm always keeping an eye out. You're my precious girl. And he's a college kid. A cute one at that."

"Okay, you can stop there. I mean, yes, he's cute but . . . that's not everything to me."

She half laughs. "Well, good. Anyway"—she hikes her hands on her hips—"shower time. We'll get to know Teddy soon enough on the mic."

I still. The mic, as in, karaoke. "We're not doing karaoke tonight . . . are we?"

Her eyebrows plunge. "It's part of our tradition. Why is this an issue? You *love* karaoke."

"Because there are strangers coming." What I don't say is that I'm almost always somehow placed on the spot to sing. Karaoke peer pressure is real. My dad will insist on a duet, like "Islands in the Stream" or "(I've Had) The Time of My Life." He'll look at me and offer his hand, and next thing I know I'm doing the snake and thinking I'm Paula Abdul.

"Strangers? Everyone has come to a family party except . . ." She pauses. "Oh . . . *Oh.*"

"No . . . no, it's not an *oh*. I just don't feel like singing in front of anyone tonight."

"But, honey," she protests.

Redirection is the key. "Shower, Mom. They'll be here in twenty minutes."

It works. She startles. "Ay nako. All right. I'll be out in about ten. Can you . . ."

"Run around and pick up? Got it."

Mom heads down the hallway and climbs the stairs, joining Dad, who's in charge of making sure the twins are dressed and all the bedrooms are clean, as if people will be partying on the second floor.

My phone buzzes in my pocket.

Teddy: We're leaving now. Are you excited?

Lila: Why would I be excited?

Teddy: Because you get to spend more time with me.

Lila: And that is a plus?

Teddy: For someone who likes Christmas books, you sure are a Scrooge.

Lila: For someone who likes nonfiction you sure like to make things up

Teddy: Burn!

I laugh. And despite my denial, the hum zipping through my body is proving that, yes, I am excited.

It's not even a half hour into dinner, and Graham and Grant excuse themselves from the table. It's my cue to stand, because sitting next to Teddy properly extinguished my appetite. The usual ease—and even the casual annoyance—I have with him is nowhere to be found. It's been replaced by my nerves, which are frayed at the edges. Our texts, the banter, our moment in the climbing gym has created an indescribable energy between us where we can't seem to look at each other.

What I can't stop ogling are his arms when he reaches for anything across the table. He's wearing a preppy long-sleeve button-down over jeans, with the sleeves rolled up. And the cologne he's wearing? *Hello.*

"Honey, is everything okay? You've barely eaten," Dad says.

"I, um . . ." Everyone's eyes are on me. "I grazed the whole time Mom cooked. I'm going to head to the living room and keep an eye on the twins."

"Good idea." Carm stands with her plate. "I'll join you."

Frank, Carm's dad, rolls his eyes. "The kids don't want to be around us. We're just not cool anymore."

"Wait till they're in college," Ms. Velasco adds. "They are literally always gone." She gives Teddy the side-eye.

I hustle away. I can't be here for this conversation. I know exactly where Teddy has been.

Once we're in the living room, Carm pushes her food around

on her plate. "So spill. What's up? I can't figure out what's wrong with you." She assesses my face. "Except maybe Teddy."

"Shh." I bump her with a shoulder.

She protects her plate. "Whoa. Watch the goods."

"Sorry, but no, it has nothing to do with him." I stab a green bean with a fork.

"Liar. Pants on fire. If you were telling me the truth, you'd look straight at me. Did something happen at the train depot?"

"Nothing happened at the train depot."

"Then why the incognito meet-up?"

"It's because . . ." Despite my need to tell her everything, I hold back. I promised Teddy. "I can't say."

"You can't say? Or won't say."

"It's . . . it's a secret." A wave of shame overcomes me.

She rocks back. "A secret?"

"And not my secret to tell." The shame is now to the third power. I have never kept a secret from Carm.

"So it's *his* secret." She frowns. "Which tells me you've gotten closer."

I shrug. She's right, in a way. From behind us, I can hear Teddy laughing with our parents. "What do you think they're talking about?"

Carm doesn't answer and instead takes a bite of her roll.

"You're upset," I say.

"I'm not upset. You're just always involved with something else. First you were involved with work, and with your blog, and now with Teddy."

Irritation rises inside me. But Carm's face is scrunched in an expression that tells me she's in no mood for debate. "What are you talking about? We saw each other every day at school, and when we've had time, we've done Mission: Holly."

"The little we've done of Mission: Holly. Which is basically one thing. You canceled on me before you started working with Teddy, then after meeting Teddy, you've done three things on the list with him."

I open my mouth to remind her that she canceled once on me too; instead, I exhale. She's right. My mind *has* been everywhere, and I haven't been following through. "I'm sorry."

Her rigid expression eases. "I'm sorry too." She turns in the seat. "I don't mean to be all clingy and dramatic, but this is our last holiday together. Who knows where we'll be next year?"

My heart picks up speed. "What are you talking about? We're going to be back here for winter break."

"I know, but what if we lose touch?" Her gaze drops to her lap. "Ugh. I'm having a hard time explaining."

"Carm?"

"Let me try again." She takes a breath. "I'm actually happy for you. Seeing you so excited around Teddy is really great. But so much is changing."

"Weren't you the one who said that change was inevitable? And what else did you say?"

"It's not all bad." Her lips curl into a grin. "I should know better than to dispense advice."

"You're actually right, though. Things are changing. I feel it in everything. I even applied for that internship yesterday."

Her face brightens. "Yeah? And how do you feel about the decision?"

"That's the thing, I don't know."

"It's okay not to know. But at least you're keeping an open mind."

"I guess." We settle into a silence. I reach for her hand and squeeze. "It's going to be our holiday, Carm."

At first she simply glances at our clasped hands. Then she looks up. "Really?"

"Really. We'll figure it out. I still have work, but we're going to conquer that list together."

"So we'll decorate cookies at Yule Be Baking?"

We did that same activity for Carm's tenth birthday. I nod.

"Can it be just the two of us?"

"That sounds perfect. Just the two of us."

"And we're still on for ice-skating at Prancer's tomorrow?"

I groan. "Me on skates is asking for trouble, but yes, I'm still down. We can invite KC if you want. His boyfriend is in town. Unless you don't—"

"I do. And I'll ask Aiden."

"Aiden, huh?" I wriggle my eyebrows at her, and she play-shoves me.

"I'll get everyone in the group chat. Maybe we can even squeeze in a couple more things during the day."

"What's up in the group chat?" Teddy comes around the couch, holding three cups of what looks like sparkling apple cider. He hands each one of us a cup and sinks into the cushion next to me. "For the dessert toast."

"Ice-skating tomorrow. Want to come with us?" Carm asks, then tips the cup to her lips.

"I think he's working." I shoot eye-daggers at her. It's one thing for me and Teddy to have this silly back-and-forth, but wholly another to make this a triple date.

"I don't need to work until tomorrow night. I love ice-skating," Teddy says.

Of course he does.

"Great! It's a plan." Carm thumbs her phone with one hand. "Teddy, give me your number and I can add you to my contacts."

While Teddy relays his number, and I'm thinking of all the ways I can torture Carm for her treachery, the squeal of the karaoke speaker catches our attention.

"Hello, hello," Graham says into the microphone. He inserts a disk into the machine.

Oh no.

Next to me, Teddy and Carm sit up straighter.

One by one, the adults bring their chairs to the living room and take a seat, each with a drink in their hand.

"As soon as Tita Lou said there would be karaoke, I was like, I can't wait," Teddy says.

"Get your lungs ready, Teddy, because this is when you get to show your stuff," Carm adds.

I press the cold cup of cider against my cheek. Ghost of Christmas Future, help me.

I'm surprised we're not visited by a neighbor complaining of a noise disturbance—we are that loud.

Correction, Teddy is that loud. He's front and center in my living room, singing "Footloose" and running in place.

"Is he high?" I say aloud, practically screaming, though only Carm has a chance of hearing me. Have I said the place is loud?

"He's just having fun!"

The music changes, and it's a duet. "Summer Nights" from the movie *Grease*.

I giggle. "Here we go."

As predicted, Mom and Dad leap to their feet like they've been waiting for this song all their lives. They both grab mics. Dad practices his scales.

The sofa whooshes next to me as Teddy sits. "I haven't done that in forever. Why haven't you gone up?"

"Don't you worry," I laugh. "No one gets away unscathed."

"This is so much fun. Dang," he says. "Are you guys always like this?"

"Chaotic?"

"Festive." His expression is open, almost vulnerable, and for a moment the rest of the room fades away. "Why are you looking at me like that?"

I avert my eyes. "What way?" But what I don't say is that, once again, Teddy has surprised me. Who knew he was a karaoke lover?

A cackle distracts him, thank goodness, and he turns his attention to his aunt, who's three sheets to the wind from sugar and is laughing so hard with Carm's parents that she's wiping away tears. "I have never seen Tita Lou this happy."

"You should hear her when she sings 'I Did It My Way.' She can hit those notes."

The house phone rings, and heads turn. "I'll get it!" Mom leaves the stage, aka in front of the television, and rushes to the kitchen. "Arturo, it's Tatang. He has a question! Sorry, guys, give us a few minutes!"

"My lolo Bob," I explain to Carm and Teddy. "In Manila."

As Dad passes us, he tosses the microphones into my and Teddy's laps. "Don't waste a perfectly good song." To Teddy he says, "Lila has a beautiful voice. She knows this song inside and out."

"Dad!"

But Dad has already pulled me to my feet. Carm cackles. Teddy saunters his way to the front.

There's no way of getting out of this. Not only have I been instructed to sing, but now everyone's expecting a performance. Irene is grinning like the devil she is—she better not record any of this, I swear.

But when Teddy sings the first line, with a grin on his face, I can't help but get into it. My body goes on autopilot. At first, my voice shakes from nervousness; it has less to do with karaoke and more to do with Teddy, who is raising the bar of this weird friendship. He's looking right into my eyes. He sways in time to the beat. Then he flips up the collar of his button-down like Danny himself, and winks.

Is it real? Is it fake? Is he simply swept up with the karaoke?

It doesn't matter, because I swoon for real, saved only by the next line of the song. For this moment, I believe him. Like I'm the girl he fell for over one summer.

Even if we are in the middle of the snow-covered Finger Lakes region at Christmastime.

Chapter 18

"Ooooh! We're almost there!" Carm says next to me. She claps her mittens together, squealing, way more excited than the kids of the family in line in front of us. We're about five feet away from the entrance of Santa's cottage.

Apparently, Santa loves Holly so much that he spends an extra couple of days with us, and taking a picture with him is tenth on the list of things to do in Holly.

If only it wasn't nine in the morning.

My eyelids are heavy from the long night. The last of our guests, Ms. Velasco and Teddy, didn't leave until after midnight. So I squint at the bright but deceiving sky, a popsicle under three layers of clothing.

"I can't believe people do this every year," I say. "I've seen the line snake around the town square."

"I know. So count your Christmas blessings that most everyone is still tucked in their bed. Oh yay!" Carm's hand shoots up. "Over here, guys!"

After a slew of apologies from familiar low voices, KC appears with who I assume is Seb. They're holding hands, and KC is positively beaming.

It's a hug fest replete with basic introductions, and we huddle closer together as we all catch up with everyone's Christmas celebrations.

KC announces, "He met the parentals."

"Aaand how did it go?" I ask.

Sebastian bites his lip, grinning. "It went all right."

"They love him, of course," KC added.

"Aw, that's great. Right, Carm?"

"Mmm-hmm." Carm's looking over my shoulder, at a guy walking in our direction. It's Aiden O'Conner. All six feet of him, in a navy-blue coat and a beanie covering his dark blond hair. "Do I look okay? Am I overdressed?" She looks down. "Maybe I wore too many layers. I mean, it will be good while we take pictures, but not for ice-skating later. Talk about a heatstroke in the making. Hey, aren't you officially certified in CPR? Do they teach heatstroke maintenance? They really should if they don't already. Oh gosh, maybe I shouldn't have invited him. He probably thinks this is all cheesy—"

"Carm!"

Her eyes dart my direction. Tendrils of hair have fallen out of her knit cap, and her cheeks are red, more from nervousness than the chill. "What?"

"Breathe!"

Her lips purse, and sure enough, she exhales just as Aiden approaches.

Then someone else sidles up to me.

I look up. It's Teddy, eyes bright. My body warms at least ten degrees.

What cold?

"You look chipper," I whisper. Beyond him staying past midnight at my house last night, we texted afterward, until I could no longer keep my eyes open.

"I sent a thirteen today," he whispers into my ear, excitement in his voice.

I have no idea what that means, but it still sends shivers through me.

As if reading my thoughts, he says, "I'll have to show you one of these days."

Now it's me who can't seem to breathe.

When we get to Santa's cottage door, the host, dressed as Santa's elf, asks, "Would you like to take a group picture, or in couples?"

"It's . . . um . . ." I look around. We are, in fact, three couples.

"I . . . uhhh," Carm adds.

"Group!" KC says, saving the moment.

We shuffle indoors, down a small corridor, toward a very realistic-looking Santa.

"He's so real, it's creepy," KC whispers.

The host elf has no time for small talk. She shuffles us next to Santa. "Some rules: no sitting on Santa's lap if you're over fifty pounds, not even in jest. All right. You go here." Host Elf pulls Carm on Santa's right, me on Santa's left, and somehow, the Elf has enough foresight to couple everyone up so that Teddy is behind me.

Host Elf skips next to Camera Elf. "All right, everyone. Get close."

Across from me, Carm giggles. And I see why. Aiden's hand is on her shoulder.

Then I feel a hand on mine.

"This okay?" Teddy asks, his face ridiculously close to mine.

My heart stutters to a stop. "Um, uh-huh."

"Ready, kids?" Santa asks. "On three, say 'Santa needs a nap!'"

"Santa needs a nap!" we say in chorus, and burst into laughter.

Except with Teddy touching me, I am now absolutely wide awake.

The picture is sent to Carm's email for future purchase and the five of us hover around her as she pulls it up. We're in line for shoes at our next Mission: Holly task, Prancer's Ice Rink, six out of six of us amped with our bellies happy after grabbing cider doughnuts at Comet's.

"Awww. That's cute!" Seb says. "We all look super happy."

"Santa knew exactly how to make us smile," Aiden says. "I heard they've hired the same Santa the last five years because he's so good."

We make it to the skate-rental counter, where each of us calls out our sizes and grabs our skates. Then we find an empty bench for all of us to sit and switch out our shoes.

"The last time I skated was when I was thirteen," Teddy says.

"I thought you said you liked ice-skating."

"I mean, I do. It's just been forever."

"You'll be in good company, because Lila sucks." Carm laughs.

I roll my eyes. "Just because you were put into ice dancing at the age of three onward."

Aiden brightens. "Ice dancing?"

"Thanks, Lila," Carm mutters.

"I'm pretty good at skating. Did some hockey growing up," KC says. "Back when I didn't care about objects hitting me at lightning speed."

"KC, Carm, if you like getting some air under your skates, you're a shoo-in for climbing," Teddy says.

I'm focusing on tying my shoes, but my ears pick up the sound of his voice, at how it lilts with happiness.

"Ready to enter the rink?" Aiden asks, standing and holding out his hand to Carm.

Carm's eyes flash with excitement, and I hope she doesn't combust. She jumps up, and they both enter the rink.

KC and Sebastian hold hands. Both look confident on skates.

It's only when they're feet away into the rink that I realize what's happened once more. Another couples situation.

My heart soars with mixed emotions. Last night, during karaoke, there was a sparkle of connection, and that small moment with Santa added to the electricity. But this is Teddy; the highs I've experienced with him are bookended with the unexpected.

I enter the rink. Seconds later, I realize that Teddy isn't with me.

I spin. He's at the rink entrance, gripping the railing. His face is a mask of fright.

Teddy, afraid? I glide, carefully, toward him.

"Okay, so it's been longer than I realized," he admits, voice shaking.

I offer my hand. "The good thing is that the distance from you to the ground is way shorter than when you're on a boulder."

"On boulders there are handholds, little cracks even. The ice is just slippery."

"You can hang on to me." I offer my second hand.

For a beat, Teddy hesitates, then reaches out, clutching one hand and prying his fingers from the wall.

"Breathe." I inhale and exhale audibly. "Now, use your abs. I know you have them—I've seen them." After the words leave my mouth, my face goes aflame. "I mean—"

But my flirtation faux pas relaxes him, and his hold on my hand eases. "Okay."

"I'm going to move backward, and you're going to skate toward me, okay?" I look up into his eyes. A hint of a smile graces his face.

I slide backward, and Teddy clomps toward me with heavy legs. "I suck at this," he says.

"I mean . . . I won't lie. I don't think I've met anyone worse than me. But we can work on it."

He nods, focused.

We continue with the pattern. Soon he's sliding more than clomping. I let go of one hand and we skate side by side.

"We're doing it." The amazement is evident in his wide smile, and it's so contagious, I can feel the cold wind against my teeth.

"You are! You're a natural!" And while I know we aren't going fast at all, in my imagination we're ice dancers in a romantic but lively routine, bound not only by our grip, but our gazes too.

From my periphery comes a shadow. It's another couple cutting in front of us, struggling to find purchase on the ice, causing Teddy to wobble.

I bear down on my skates to slow us down. His arms flail; I try to steady his torso. His hands land on my shoulders, and we tip.

"Whoa!" he yelps.

"Steady," I command, more to myself than to him, and force

my skates down against the ice. And after a few seconds, his thrashing calms, and he lets out a booming laugh.

We still as we both realize what has happened. We are clutching on to one another. Our faces are inches apart. So close that our breaths mingle.

"Oh my God. That was wild," he says. His voice is low, and it rumbles through me, momentarily taking my breath away.

"I can't believe we didn't wipe out."

"It's because of you. I feel like all you do is try to help me."

The statement is both vulnerable and sweet. It hits me right in the heart. "Are you admitting that I haven't been nagging, but helping?"

He laughs. "I plead the Fifth . . ." His gaze drops to my lips, and in that short moment, a thought skitters through me. That it feels good to be this close. That maybe he'll kiss me. "Lila—"

He's interrupted by Ms. Velasco's ringtone in my jacket pocket. It's like the gong of the town square's bell at midnight, and the high of the moment plummets.

"It's your tita," I say.

He frowns. "You should get it. It's probably about work."

I do, but it means I have to let go of Teddy. It's like ripping off a Band-Aid. "Hello?"

"Lila?" Ms. Velasco's voice is a screech of panic. "Are you with Teddy by chance? He mentioned ice-skating with you and your friends."

"He's here with me."

"Good, then this will be one message for the both of you. Could the two of you come in when you can? We've got four who called in sick."

I raise my chin to Teddy. "Four people called out at the Inn. Ms. Velasco needs us to cover."

He nods.

"We'll head in right away."

"Oh thank God. I'll see you soon."

I hang up and clear my throat. Whatever was there between me and Teddy is gone; still, I brave a question. "What were you going to say before she called?"

Something passes before his eyes. "Just . . . thanks."

"Of course." I don't know what I expected, but a part of me wished it was more.

"We should go, huh?" He looks longingly at the exit.

"Do you need help to get there?"

"If you don't mind." Half of his face scrunches into a wince.

"C'mon, Teddy, let's go." I giggle and take his hand, leading him to the exit. But this time, I remind myself that we're just friends.

Chapter 19

After I swing home to change into my uniform, update my mom, and pack myself a snack, I head back out into the afternoon. Like usual, the Inn is packed. Cars line the side of the road on the long driveway leading to the Bookworm Inn, and it takes me a couple of rounds circling the parking lot before a space becomes free.

The snow is steady and each flake is heavy and wet. For the first time in forever, Mr. Weather from KHLY is right: He called for steady snow through the afternoon and heavy snow in the evening.

But Mr. Weather doesn't prepare me for the chaos inside.

The gift shop is packed to the brim, and it's *hot*. I spot Teddy at the register. In addition to his polo shirt, he's wearing a Santa hat. It jingles every time his head moves, and it's so adorable.

Upon closer inspection, however, I realize Teddy is far from jolly. He's sweating, his hands moving quickly across the register. Another green sweater darts by—I miss who it is—and a child in the store cries. Someone barks out a laugh, and another person sneezes.

It's going to be a rough night.

I slip in behind Teddy once I've dumped all my stuff in the break room, and after exchanging a silent hello, I jump on the second register.

Two people come toward me. Both are grandma types who try to beat each other to the counter. I already have my hands up as they approach. One never underestimates the determination of lolas, Filipino or otherwise. "Ladies, I can only take one at a time."

"I got here first," says the grandma in red.

"That's because you cut me," says the one in green, pointing along the left side of the register with her cane.

"Well, that's your problem. That isn't the line. *This* is the line." Grandma in red points toward the ground where there are arrows on the floor, marked by red duct tape.

"We have arrows?" It takes me aback. It's only been four days since my last shift.

"I taped them down the other day to divert folks so they don't clump up right in the middle," Teddy says while packing up a T-shirt.

"Wow," I say. I'm reminded of the different-colored footholds in the climbing gym. "That's not a bad idea."

"Thanks." He looks at me, hanging on a beat longer than usual.

Butterflies stir in my belly.

"So, it's me who's first." Grandma in red yanks me out of my thoughts.

I nod belatedly, then turn to the grandma with the cane. "I apologize for the wait, but if you can move back to the arrow, I can help you next after this customer."

Grandma with the cane grumbles but does as I request.

Indeed, after the initial confusion, the arrows help with the crowd. And despite my wandering thoughts, and the occasional brush against Teddy while behind the counter, I focus enough to manage the long lines and stock inventory.

"Do you know about the snowstorm that's supposed to roll in tonight?" says the customer in front of me with a Southern accent and a cowgirl hat. She only has one thing in her basket: a magnet. "I'm planning on grabbing a ton of water tonight, in case we get snowed in."

Here's the thing about the snow up north. What others might think is a snowstorm is, simply, heavy snow. A true snowstorm cuts out power and roads. In the Finger Lakes, our power grid can handle snowfall. Our snowplowers are the best in the business, making sure our roads are clear at all hours of the night and day. School is hardly ever canceled. "Oh yeah?" I say anyway, just to keep the conversation moving. "That will be six dollars and one cent."

She hands me ten dollars. "This place has been the absolute best. I'm sad I won't be here for the event on New Year's Eve. I was a day late for tickets." She declines a bag. "Jonah Johanson is such a dreamboat."

"I agree." I sigh and wave to the customer. To Teddy, I whisper-scream, "Did you hear that? Tickets are sold out. I'm so glad my mom got tickets for us."

"Do you really think Jonah Johanson is a dreamboat?" he asks.

I wave another customer over. "What do you mean?"

"You totally blushed."

As I scan the customer's things, I bite back a grin. "Jonah Johanson was voted the sexiest man alive by *People* in 1998."

"Yes, he was," says the customer with a smile. He swipes his credit card. "I still have the copy."

"See?" I point out. Carefully, I wrap the wooden backscratcher with the movie quote etched with *Scratch my back? No way!* in tissue.

Teddy frowns. "He's like . . . a dad."

"Yeah, so?" I tease as I pack the backscratcher in a bag. To the customer, I say, "Thank you so much for coming to the Bookworm Inn."

"I'd call him Daddy," the customer says with a nod, and leaves with his things.

Teddy's mouth drops open in shock.

I cackle so hard now it's me who's sweating.

Two swift hours later, we serve our very last customer. After Teddy turns off the automatic doors, we both lean back against the glass and heave a breath.

"Wow," he says.

"Whoa," I answer back, surveying the damage left by today's visitors.

The gift shop is a mess. Random receipts and trash litter the floor. Somebody took a liking to the magnets on the six-foot display and stacked them flat, one on top of the another. And in every small circular clothing display, hangers stick out like barbed wire.

Teddy and I look at each other. His hair is disheveled; white cotton fuzz from the Christmas village snow sticks on his uniform sweater. My sweater has a couple of price stickers attached to it, and the patch logo on my upper chest hangs by a thread thanks to an eager baby who was handed to me when their mommy needed to use the bathroom.

We both crack up.

"That. Was. Madness," I say.

"I have never, ever witnessed anything that chaotic. What did I even do that whole time?"

"You did everything, Teddy. And pretty well, actually."

"Are you just saying that so you can thank my teacher?"

"That's actually a stellar idea." I reach to pat myself on the back, but groan. My arms are sore, and my cheeks hurt from all the smiles for customers and from laughs with Teddy—I haven't had that much fun working in forever. "But seriously, the arrows on the floor? The complimentary samples of the Bookworm Inn boxed chocolates? It was genius. After you thought of passing them out, they flew right off the shelves. Your strategy worked."

"Someone told me once that a way to a customer's heart is through their eyes. And I thought, why not open the box for them to see what's really in it?"

I warm at the thought that Teddy actually listened to me. "That was all you. But thanks."

"I didn't get to say it earlier, but . . . . I had a good time ice-skating and taking pictures with Santa. And at karaoke."

This time, my groan is deep and regretful. "We don't have to talk about karaoke."

"But, Sandy—"

I laugh. "Shut up!"

"No seriously, you were so good."

"Thanks." And yet, suspicion nags at me. "What's up?"

"What do you mean what's up?"

"That was a compliment sandwich. I'm waiting for the bread."

He throws his head back in laughter. And maybe it's the furnace kicking in, but a warm flush starts in my toes, rushes straight up my torso, and then up my neck.

Teddy rests a hand behind his head and dips his chin to his chest. "Now that you mention it . . ."

The warmth halts at the level of my chin. I sense that someone needs a favor. "Let me guess, you need for me to take a shift."

"Yeah, actually. The thirtieth. Tita Lou just put up the schedule and I've got—"

"—practice for your competition."

He nods. "It's coming up close, and I want to spend as much time climbing as I can. Will you do it? We can switch shifts."

I heave a breath, but I don't actually mind. The last few days brought our relationship to another level, to real friendship.

"I don't have any shifts to switch," I say.

"I'll owe you one?" He raises his hand for a high five. "I'm good for it."

I roll my eyes and slap his hand.

"You're the best. Yesss," he says.

Our hands fall, still intertwined. My gaze drops down to our linked fingers. He's still holding on. *I'm* still holding on.

And his hands are warm, calloused, and strong. This is the first time we've really touched. Not glove to glove, not hand to carabiner, or hand to shoulder. But skin to skin.

His eyes are rounded, startled. But neither of us lets go. And, after the initial shock, it feels right. Comfortable.

Voices snatch our attention. At the sound of footsteps, we jump back. I find myself in front of the flimsy souvenir sunglasses. As I rearrange the inventory, I brave a final glance at Teddy, who's working on separating the magnets. I wish a pair of these sunglasses could render me invisible.

Ms. Velasco enters with a familiar face—Kira Mahoney, Jonah Johanson's PR person. Their smiles are as bright Rudolph's nose.

I feel like a voyeur, peeking out from behind the display. But I don't want to disrupt them. In my periphery, Teddy is silent too.

Until the magnets he's arranging fall to the ground, making a clacking noise.

"Oh!" Ms. Velasco scans the floor. "Teddy? Lila?"

We both inch away from our hiding places and head toward them.

"Hi!" I wave. "Hi, Kira."

Teddy does a halfhearted salute.

Ms. V looks just as flustered as we feel. "Thanks to both of you for stepping into the shift."

"Yeah, sure." But what I'm curious about is Kira's presence. What can I say? I'm nosy. "Is there news about the event?"

"Actually, yes." With a short and sweet glance at Kira, she says, "We've been ironing out the schedule. Took a little bit with coordinating arrival and departure times, and of course the staffing we would need."

"But we have it down now," Kira adds.

"Can you share?" I clasp my hands against my chest. I'm just short of getting on my knees and pleading.

"The actors will participate in a panel. Then we'll have fireworks, and a special book and swag signing. We're expecting the daughter of the late author to come represent the author camp."

My jaw drops at this, and tears prick my eyes. "Wow, that's so special."

"Well, I'd better get on the road," Kira says. "We're supposed to get dumped on tonight, and I want to beat the snow."

"Thank you again for stopping by," Ms. Velasco says. Right then, if I could put an emoji to her expression, it would be heart eyes. "I'll walk you out."

"Of course. Nice to see you both again, Teddy and Lila."

After a round of goodbyes, Kira and Ms. V head to the back exit.

"Okay, you can roll up that tongue and put it back in your mouth," Teddy says.

"How could you not sit there and absorb the greatness?"

He snickers. "She's the PR rep to the stars, not a star herself."

"That's pretty dang close."

"And," he continues, "Jonah and Remy are just people."

"Teddy. Remy Castillo has survived Hollywood. And she looks like us. You saw the film. She was amazing in it."

He shrugs and fusses with the tabletop display of lip balms.

"Wait a sec, you still haven't watched the movie?" When he doesn't answer, I press, "Did you at least read the book?"

He shakes his head, and the expression on his face loses its playfulness; his lips thin into a serious expression. "I'm too busy climbing. I have a competition, remember? Which is much more important than an old movie. In fact, I need to go to sleep. Let's get this place cleaned up."

"Oh, so now you're being responsible?" I tease.

He counters with a deadpan expression. "I did learn from the best."

Something is up. He's acting like old Teddy again. "What's up with you?"

"Nothing." He bends down to pick up merchandise from the

floor. "It's late, and I've got an early morning. Time me, Santos. We'll be out of here in an hour."

"Fine." But he doesn't hear my answer, because he's already left my side.

Count out register—check
Wipe down counters—check
Complete go-backs—check
Tidy up break room—check
Vacuum—check

"So?" Teddy stares at me in earnest, holding a dust rag. "All done?"

I look up from the laminated list. "I think so."

A grin splits his face. "Ha—didn't I call it? I called it. One hour."

And despite my best efforts not to inflate his ego, I say, "You called it. You were right."

"Am I the fastest closer at the Bookworm Inn or what?"

"This is ridiculous. I haven't closed with everyone." Then I raise a finger. "Wait. I have closed with everyone. Still, the point is ridiculous."

"Ridiculous but right."

When Teddy is motivated, he is an entirely different person. His brief sullen mood earlier has disappeared. Not once did he and I argue during closing, nor did he question anything on the checklist. "Now if you were this agreeable from the start, things could have been different."

"I like to keep people on their toes." He lifts the rag. "I'll put this away and lock up. Where did you park?"

"At the entrance to the parking lot."

"I'll walk you out, then. I've got my boots with me."

"You don't have to, but okay. See you at the back door." I grab my things and turn off the lights. It's just past ten p.m., and there's still enough time to get home and type up my next blog post in the peace and quiet.

Teddy waits for me at the back exit, which he's opened to the white expanse of the parking lot. There are solid inches of snow on the ground. The wheels of Ms. Velasco's car, parked next to the Inn, are half buried, and the flakes continue to fall like a sheer curtain.

"Crap." It's going to be a slippery drive home.

"Let me go grab a shovel." Teddy disappears toward the Inn.

I slip on my winter boots and step out onto the pathway. The snow gives with the slightest touch, which is a good sign.

The door creaks behind me, and I turn. "The snow isn't bad. Just some drift."

"Actually." It's Ms. Velasco at the door instead of Teddy. "I got a call that we have a couple of felled trees. Jamie and Lina, who are trying to come up the hill to work the night shift, can't get through. We've got to wait for Clyde to get up here and move the trees before you can go down the hill, but he says it will be about three hours."

Clyde works the Inn's landscaping.

"Oh no." There goes my night.

"I'm sorry, honey. Do you want me to call your parents to say you'll be late? You're probably super tired. Maybe I can put you in a room . . . Oh darn." She bites her lip.

I come to the same conclusion at the same time she does.

"All of our rooms are booked," she says. "I'd say stay in our cabin, but it's quite tight in there with me and Teddy and his things. But you can hang out in the gift shop if you'd like. It's safe, and you can lock the door, watch movies to pass the time until Clyde can clear the driveway." The door opens and Teddy appears behind her. "Can you wait with Lila? Now that Jaime and Lina can't come in, I'm on duty for the first part of the night. We're short as it is, and we've got a full house."

"Yeah, of course, Tita Lou."

She wraps her arms around Teddy's shoulders. "I'm so lucky you're here with me this winter. You've saved me more times than I can count, even if I don't know where you are half the time."

Teddy looks at his feet. "It's all good, Tita."

"Same here," I add.

Her shoulders round in relief. "Thank you both for under-standing." She leans in to hug me and Teddy at the same time. "When you're both at Syracuse, you'll have to make sure to come visit me often. I'll miss you both."

Chapter 20

Ms. Velasco's words don't catch up to me until I'm inside.

When you're both at Syracuse, you'll have to make sure to come visit me often.

When Teddy first arrived at the Bookworm Inn, I'd categorized him as a seasonal worker, someone who's here temporarily, when there's actually a great possibility that I will see him after this winter.

If I can afford Syracuse, that is.

It puts all the emotions I feel for him in a different context. It's like the first snowfall of the year—full of potential.

The clang of metal grabs my attention. Teddy walks in carrying two folded padded chairs under one arm and pillows and blankets under the other. "Courtesy of the Bookworm Inn. Tita Lou was worried that the break room chairs weren't comfortable to sit on. You can use one as an ottoman. And blankets in case you get cold."

"Thank you. I've got it from here," I offer. "You've got stuff to do."

"No way. Tita would kill me if she knew I didn't make sure you were good." He rushes ahead to the free library area. "Do you mind if I push this table out of the way?"

"I'm totally fine with that." But I'm more than fine. To be honest, I'm touched that he thought to ask. "This is a perfect spot."

He stuffs his hands in his pockets after he sets up the chairs. "So whatcha gonna do while you wait?"

I gesture to my backpack. "You know me, I can keep busy."

"You have a book in there, don't you?"

"But of course. And I have my phone, which is another reading device."

"And you can blog from it."

I eye him.

He laughs. "We're seriously alone. No one's going to know."

"Fine. Yes. I am going to blog."

"I'm interested to see what Christmas story you read next. Who knew there were holiday cozy mysteries and thrillers? Not just the romances everyone knows about."

"Sometimes it's hard to choose, with so many indie and self-pubbed books in addition to books published by big publishing houses." I peer at him. "Wait a sec. How many of my posts have you read?"

"Um . . . most."

"Most?" My face heats.

"Okay, all. I mean, if you're going to start a blog, isn't that what it's for? For people to read it?"

"I . . ." Of course, I know that. I *knew* that. "I don't usually discuss my blog with anyone."

"I guess it would make sense, since you're keeping it a secret."

He runs a hand through his hair. "I like your blog's format. You ask great questions. They get to the heart of the book. Also, I love your pros and cons. I like how you categorize the sidebar, so I can go straight to genre. It's . . . organized, much like you. I actually picked up a couple of books you recommended."

This fact makes my brain go fuzzy. "You picked up books I recommended?"

"Yeah, I sent gift ebooks to my mom for Christmas."

Here's the thing, in the twenty-three months I've blogged, I have never really seen the result of it. Yes, I get the comments on my posts. But I've never had someone, in person, tell me that I've helped them pick out a book.

I'm flummoxed. I don't know what to do with this information. "That's . . . nice." I wince at my lack of articulate words. "I'm actually really honored."

His phone in his hand lights up. Moment over.

"I guess I should go?" He takes a step back. But he hesitates, like he doesn't want to.

The question in his tone spurs me forward. I like that he's waiting for a sign from me.

"Unless . . ." I look at my phone. "I mean, do you want to hang out? I know you have to climb in the morning."

"I do have practice, but I can move it."

"Okay." But inside, I'm anything but okay. We're alone, and my feelings for him are stronger than ever, and what do I do with that?

The heater clicks on, and the icicle lights we put up sway from the blast of the warm vent air. It spurs an idea.

"Are you still down for doing something for Mission: Holly?"

He brightens. "Yeah, sure."

"By all means, have a seat." I gesture to one of the chairs. "Close your eyes."

His eyebrows lift.

"Do you trust me?"

Slowly, he shuts his eyes. "Yes," he says without hesitation.

His answer awakens the butterflies in my belly. I gulp.

In my silence he adds, "I mean, you did catch me while ice-skating."

I smile. "Keep them shut." I turn the corner of the nearest bookshelf and pick out the perfect thing that will pass the time. I pluck it out of its case and slip it into the gift shop's entertainment system. With the remote control, I press PLAY.

The iconic intro from *Holiday by the Lake* fills the room.

"Nooooo," Teddy says, opening his eyes. He doubles over as if in pain and groans. "This isn't on the Mission: Holly list is it?"

"It is now!" I laugh, and physically push him until he finally sits up. "It's not that bad."

"What is it with this movie? It's so predictable. And pure emotional manipulation." He gestures to the framed movie poster hanging across from us.

Yet, despite his reaction, I don't take the bait. This is a person who has been reading my holiday book recommendations. He's way more open-minded than he lets on.

I keep my face neutral. As an eldest sister, patience is a skill that I have mastered. I click the stop button on the remote control and the scene freezes to the aerial view of Holly. "How about we flip for it?"

His eyes round, excitement beaming through. "All right." He jumps up and lumbers to the cash registers, to our penny jar.

Upon returning, he presents the penny in his palm. "Do you want to do the honors?"

"Sure," I say, taking it. The penny is marred and darkened in some places, but Abraham Lincoln's profile is shiny. C'mon, Abe. We got this. "You call it."

As I flip the penny in the air, Teddy says, "Tails."

I snatch the penny and keep it in my grasp. "Ready?"

"You're intense even down to this coin toss." He smirks. "But I love it. Let's see it."

I slap the coin into my palm and slowly withdraw my hand. It's heads.

"No no no, don't leave!" Teddy slaps his palm against his forehead. He gestures toward the screen, at the young Leo Marks, who's walking away from a sobbing Estelle Mendoza.

It's the lowest, saddest point in the movie, and a part of me wants to spoil the ending for Teddy, to end his torture. What he doesn't know is that a happily-ever-after awaits. But I bite my cheek to keep myself from spilling. I want to witness his reaction.

While the writing has room for improvement, the acting is spot on. There's a reason why new, skeptical viewers like Teddy are hooked despite their initial resistance, and why it has been such a special part of our town for so many years—Jonah Johanson and Remy Castillo brought it. Readers of the book and viewers of the film want the happily-ever-after for these characters. And with the triumphant ending, it makes people feel that they can get their own happily-ever-after.

For all of his talk about not wanting to watch this movie, Teddy now has a pillow clutched to his chest. And somehow, our chairs are pushed together and our shoulders and thighs are touching.

"I can't. I can't." He presses PAUSE so the screen freezes on the shot of the heartbroken Estelle walking down Main Street, which is lit up by festive blinking colorful lights. Teddy's expression is incredulous. "How could he walk away, after . . . after she said that she loved him?"

"I guess you're going to have to watch the rest of it," I cajole. "Have faith."

He heaves a breath. When he does, his hair flops forward. "I'm going to raid the break room for snacks. I need sustenance. Is that okay?"

I nod. But more than that, I love that he's so invested. It's like finding out someone likes the same book you do—it creates an instant bond. In this case, it strengthens it. "It's so good, right?"

"If you mean stress-inducing, then yes." He stands. "I'll be back with food."

As soon as Teddy disappears around the corner, I check in with Carm via text. I'd updated her on my status after I called my parents, and I'm bursting with both news and curiosity. She and Aiden ended up hanging out after ice-skating.

> **Carm:** You kept me on read for forever!
> What are you guys doing?

> **Lila:** Watching Holiday by the Lake

> **Carm:** And what else?

Lila: Aaaaaand that's it.
What are you doing?

Carm: None of your beeswax.

Lila: CARM

Carm: LILA
Okay, so Aiden came over
to watch a movie here too

Lila: With Frank and Trish?

Carm: Yes it was fully embarrassing

Lila: So does that mean . . .

Carm: I have no idea

"Yes," Teddy cheers from the break room. He must have found the secret stash of popcorn. First comes the crinkling of the wrapper and then the beep of the microwave. It makes me smile, his sudden bursts of enthusiasm.

Carm: So . . . I think it's time for
you to finally admit it.

Lila: Admit what.

Carm: That, sweet Lila, you like him.

I shake my head at the phone, but I know my best friend is right.

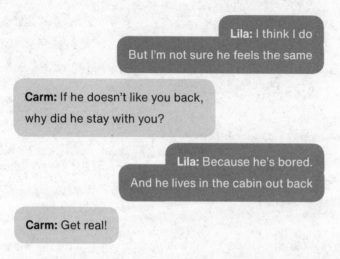

Lila: I think I do
But I'm not sure he feels the same

Carm: If he doesn't like you back,
why did he stay with you?

Lila: Because he's bored.
And he lives in the cabin out back

Carm: Get real!

The smell of popcorn filters into the room, and my stomach growls. It's followed by Teddy, holding the steaming bag. He tosses a kernel into his mouth. "I think I'm ready to tackle the end of this movie." He sits down next to me. "It ends well, right? No one dies?"

"No," I laugh. "No one dies."

"Just making sure. Sometimes you just need a happy ending." He echoes my words from my last blog post and offers the bag. "Want some?"

"Sure," I say, keeping a smile from leaving my lips. I'd like a happily-ever-after too.

Chapter 21

As we watch the credits roll, blinking lights shine into the window.

"Clyde's here!" I stand and watch the snowplow crest the hill into the parking lot. When I turn around, Teddy is still sitting there with the empty bag of popcorn on his lap. He looks bereft, and once more my heart squeezes at his reaction. "What did you think?"

"Okay, so you were right," he says. "It's a good movie."

"Told you so."

"I can see why this whole place is revered." He sighs, and his face falls into a frown.

"You okay?" I sit back down.

"Yeah. I . . . Never mind."

"No, what is it?"

"I was just thinking how I haven't taken this place seriously. My parents always say that Tita Lou bites off more than she can chew, especially after inheriting this place from Lola. Did you know that there was an offer for the business when Lola died?"

I shake my head.

"Someone wanted to buy the entire property, the concept, everything, but Tita Lou refused. My mom, on the other hand, was ready to let it go. But this place was left to the both of them. They fought about it, and in the end, Tita Lou bought my mom out."

"Wow. That's why—" I start, then back off.

He half laughs. "Why I was pretty negative? Yeah. But you made sure that I checked my preconceived notions. And now I'm looking at this whole place, at Tita Lou even, with new eyes. And maybe my mom's issue with her shouldn't be mine."

My mother's words from our Leftover Christmas dinner return to me: *I want the both of you to be close, through the ups and downs. Family is all we have.*

"You have to understand," he continues, "my parents are serious people. Not only are they serious, but they're also risk averse. Going into business like this—it doesn't guarantee success."

"This place is a success."

"I know . . . just not in their eyes."

"Is that why you don't want to tell them about your climbing?"

"No." He sighs. "I hate to talk about this, because it makes everyone worry."

From the look on his face, I can tell this is no laughing matter. "You don't have to tell me."

"No, I want to. You know everything else. I've . . . I've had a couple of concussions."

"A couple?" Alarm rings through me. I think about the news segments I've seen on TBI. "That doesn't sound good."

"No, and they're both from climbing."

The memory of him climbing that sky-high wall returns, but this time, I picture the frightening image of him falling . . .

I clutch my stomach. "God, that must have been horrible."

"I was on a boulder. The funny thing about it is that I was only five feet off the ground."

I shake my head. "I don't think that's funny at all."

"No, you're right. It wasn't. It was a novice competition, when I was younger, in middle school. Not too hard for what I could have accomplished at that time. But I was arrogant. That day, I lost focus. I was coming from underneath"—he looks up and pretend-clutches the air, and for a moment, I see exactly what he was doing—"and it was a simple push off with my left foot to get my hand to the next handhold and . . ."

His hands drop to his lap.

I wince at the image.

"I should have landed on my feet, but I was expecting to make it. My back and head took the brunt. I recovered from it after about a month. Then I fell again—we all realize now that it was too early for me to go back—and my parents pulled the plug. I don't know about you, but when someone takes the thing you love away, it's a rough go. As soon as I left for college, the first thing I did was look for the nearest climbing gym." His eyebrows knit together. "And now I . . ."

"What is it?"

"My parents think I'm at school for winter classes. But I used that as an excuse so that I could keep climbing and enter this competition."

"Wait." The words settle in my brain. "Your parents don't know you're in Holly?"

He rubs the back of his head. "No. And Tita Lou and my mom don't talk to one another, so . . ."

"That's . . ."

"It's lying to the nth degree. And I'm not proud of it." He leans into his elbows, then looks back up at me. "You're judging me, aren't you?"

I catch his gaze. It's not judgment I have, but empathy. To me, Teddy and climbing are synonymous. It's his passion. "I'm not here to do that. I have my own secrets, remember?"

"You know, Lila, you should be telling the world that you're Tinsel and Tropes." Then, after a beat, his shoulders drop. "Then again, who am I to say, right? I haven't owned up to my secrets. Although . . . I plan to tell my parents before the competition."

"You do?"

He nods. "I've been thinking of the perfect time, but it hasn't come up yet. Though I doubt they'll want to support me after I tell them. I guess I didn't plan out this far."

"Listen, Teddy . . ." I take a breath and say what I would want to be said to me. "No matter what, I'll be there for you."

"You mean that?"

"Yeah, I do."

A silence follows, and in that space, I realize that our friendship has grown leaps and bounds since our truce at the train depot. And despite our rough start, I accept him. I trust him.

It gives me the courage to share. "I don't know what to do." The words plop out of my mouth. "I mean . . ." I try again. "I thought I knew what I wanted to do. It seemed clear—to be in a career that would make me successful and financially comfortable. I'm good at science. I'm good with people. So why not a doctor? And yet—"

"You're not feeling that way now?"

"No. Yes. I don't know. It's what I put down on my college applications. It's what I've told everyone. I got footed pajamas with stethoscopes on them for Christmas."

"Those sound fun." He leans back in his seat.

"They are. And it's not as if I'm against the idea of being a doctor. I came up with it when . . ." I swallow the nerves creeping up my esophagus. My first instinct is to keep all of this in; after all, opportunity comes from struggle, and what's done is done. But Teddy has been honest with me. Now it's my turn.

So I press on. "I blog anonymously not to keep my identity secret from the rest of the world, but to keep it from my parents."

"Your parents don't know?"

I shake my head.

"They don't want you to write?"

"No. I mean, it's not that they don't want me to write." I shift in my chair, not from discomfort but to get my facts in order. "Four winters ago, there was an accident with my dad's business," I begin, and tell Teddy everything. The HelpFund, the doxing, the prank phone calls. The creepy guy. My parents' rules. As I share, the weight on my shoulders decreases a smidge, and it allows me to dive into what it all means to me, today. "I'm sure my parents are digging their way out of it still, though they don't complain. With so many of us kids, it has to be hard, right? I don't want to be a burden. I want to help them in the future. Being a doctor, I thought, would get me there."

"But you don't think so anymore?"

I shrug. "Being a doctor should allow me to help them and my siblings. But can other things do that too? I've thought about it so much during the break that I even filled out an internship application for something that's not remotely associated with premed."

He brightens, and with the curl of his lips, I can't help but smile too. "You did?"

"Yeah. But, you see, nothing can come out of it. Even if I got in, which is a long shot, I can't accept. What am I going to do? Tell my parents that I've been lying to them for two years? It's a mess. *I'm* a mess."

He rests a hand on my wrist. "Don't say that. You're far from it. You . . . You're someone I admire."

I peer at him, though inside, my heart has swelled three sizes. "What do you *really* want, Rivera? Are you asking me for another shift switch?"

"No, I mean it." He laughs. "I ran away from home just so I could climb. And you—"

"I'm hiding things too."

"But you're still doing what you need to do with your family, with work. And you're so loyal to this town. To this Inn, to my tita, And even to that freaking movie." He gestures to the television.

I blush. "Well . . . thanks."

The bells of the back door ring, halting our conversation. I exhale. It's as if I've unloaded bricks off my shoulders. Like writing a blog post times one hundred, where I don't realize I had so much to say until it's all on the screen.

"Lila?" Ms. Velasco enters, then stops short. "Teddy, you've been here all this time?"

"Kept her company like you asked," he answers.

"We were watching *Holiday by the Lake*," I proudly say.

She smiles, though it doesn't quite make it to her eyes; she's exhausted. "That's great. Clyde . . . He's cleared the path, so you're safe to get down the hill."

"Yeah, I saw. I'll clean up here and be on my way."

Her gaze slides over to Teddy. "I have to get back to the Inn, but—"

"I'll help clean up," Teddy supplies.

"Lila, I'll see you at the event, right?"

"Yes. Mom's got the tickets in our safe."

Ms. Velasco laughs.

"You'll see her before then, because she's working for me on the thirtieth. Remember, Lila?" Teddy says.

"That's right, I am."

"Why can't you take your shift, Teddy?" Ms. Velasco's forehead crinkles.

"I'm meeting up with some friends."

"Again?"

"Yep." Teddy looks away.

The conversation trails to an awkward silence, but finally Ms. Velasco bids us goodbye. As soon as the door closes behind her, I comment, "She seemed upset."

He puts away the movie. "It's not you, it's me. You're right about what you said earlier. I haven't been easy to live with, and she's probably worried that I'm corrupting you. But if she only knew." He heads to the back door.

I turn out the lights so the only things on are the twinkle lights on the window. "Knew what?"

"That, if anything, being with you has changed me, for the better."

Stunned by Teddy's comment, I step outside without my coat. "Oh, wait I—"

"I'll get it." He pops back into the gift shop and with a gush of warm air, reappears with my coat. He holds it open for me. "Here, you've got your hands full."

I slip into my coat one arm at a time, mulling over his words; then, he helps me hike up my backpack. But as we step off the curb, the cold slams into me like a wall of ice and I shiver, wishing I'd taken the time to button up. The keys in my hand fall to the ground as I attempt to pull up my hood.

"Got it," Teddy says, bending down. He must have thick skin because he's only wearing a windbreaker and thin knit gloves.

As he stands and hands me my keys, he frowns. "Your teeth are chattering. Here. Can I—" He gestures to my open coat, and I nod.

But before he buttons me up, he takes the two sides of my coat and tugs them closed. A silent gasp escapes my lips. The act is like having his arms wrap tightly around me.

His gaze is unflinching and I cannot look away.

"I liked getting to know you, Lila," he says as he buttons my coat. The deftness of his fingers ratchets up the heat inside me. I am a marshmallow melting over fire.

I've always been risk-averse. But in this moment, in this cold, snowy night, I want to take a chance.

So I reach out and rest my hands on his waist, bravery surging through me. In the nonchalant tone he's so good at, I say, "I guess you haven't been so bad to hang out with, either."

Teddy stills. The last button slips through the buttonhole. He steps in and cocoons me in his arms, for real. "Is that right?"

"Has anyone ever told you that you talk a lot while watching movies?"

He barks out a laugh. "No."

"Well, you do. Next time I'm going to make sure you have popcorn from the start." I bite my lip.

"Next time?" he whispers.

I nod.

He fingers a flyaway strand of hair and tucks it behind my ear. At this sweet gesture, I draw closer to him, just as he trails a thumb down the side of my cheek. The moment settles into an easy silence.

It's like every romance I ever read. It's *Holiday by the Lake* but better because this is real, and Teddy is . . . Teddy is completely different than I had ever expected.

"Can I kiss you?" His voice is raspy, and the question is like tinsel on a perfectly decorated tree. Like plump berries hanging from mistletoe. Tempting.

"Yes," I whisper.

I rise up to my tiptoes and shut my eyes.

When his lips feather against mine, I'm infused with energy and thrill. My hands climb his back, his cup my face, and he kisses me as if I'm another puzzle he has to explore.

I've never been kissed like this before.

Teddy pulls away first, gently, and I land back on my heels, breathing heavily.

I'm catching up to my brain when I hear the town square's bell ringing. It's one in the morning.

"I'd better go," I say.

"I'll walk you." He keeps his arms around me as we trudge to my car. I don't feel the cold, just his body against mine.

He opens the car door for me, and I slip inside and turn on the engine. I've got so many questions bubbling in the back of my mind—like, what will tomorrow bring?—but I push them all away. I'm almost always thinking about the consequences of the past as well as preparing for the future. Right now, I want to stay in the present.

"This was a great night," he says, bending down at my car door.

"Even the movie?"

"Yeah, even the movie."

"I thought for sure you were going to cry at the end." I gaze up at him. Despite my tummy twisting and turning at his closeness, there's no awkwardness between us.

"I almost did. That scene with her dog—that was rough. But the movie was completely eclipsed by you."

I bite my lip.

"And that. That is so dang cute." He bends down and catches my lips in his. "I want to kiss you every time you bite your lip." Then, in a smooth move, he pulls the seat belt around me and locks me in.

My breath leaves my body. "You and your belts and straps."

"You know it," he says with a laugh. "I'll text you. Good night."

By the time I pull into my driveway, there's already a text from Teddy: *Hang out with me today?*

I don't think twice: *Yes*

TINSEL AND TROPES
A HOLIDAY BOOK BLOG

Title: The Christmas Dare by Dahlia Nguyen
GENRE/CATEGORY: ADULT PSYCHOLOGICAL THRILLER

What aren't you willing to do?

In this holiday thriller set during a hostage situation—replete with candy canes, Christmas cookies, and a comical main character with an addiction to gingerbread lattes—our main character is dared to sabotage Christmas in her town, or else her secret is revealed. The book spans twenty-four hours, and with every strike of the clock, she must decide if the dare is worth keeping her secret—before time runs out.

What a mind game of a book, for us and for the main character! This combination of holiday joy with literal bombs, stalking, and impending death (By the way, the author posts content warnings here. Thank you, author!) was, at times, difficult to figure out how I felt about it. But when I say that this book is tropetastic, I'm not kidding. There is kidnapping, a secret identity, and an antihero whose goodness emerges through the magic of the holiday spirit. The pace doesn't let up, and I did not take a breath until The End.

It makes me wonder what I'm willing to risk for a secret. And, here's the thing, since secrets come out anyway, were any of the main characters' sacrifices worth it in the end?

Pros: Perfect with a gingerbread latte.

Cons: It's quite dark! Just saying.

Recommended for: Those who are willing to forgo bedtime. This was a page-turner!

Rating: 4 stars

Chapter 22

"Earth to Ate Lila. Hellooo." Irene's voice cuts through the fog of my thoughts. I shake myself and resume flipping pancakes. After getting home after one in the morning and writing up a quick blog post, I took what was basically just a short nap, then woke to the house in a flurry.

My entire family is here: Us kids are still on break, Mom is off the clock for the next twenty-four hours (which means she's determined to spend the day with us), and Dad's not due at work until 10:00 a.m. "Lean on Me," the karaoke version, echoes through the house—because Christmas lasts the full twelve days here—and behind the instrumental is Dad's voice and my brothers' yelps.

For some people, this would be considered chaos, but for me, usually, it's white noise.

Except when you've only gotten what feels like four hours of sleep; then it is plain old annoying.

From the kitchen island, Irene scrunches her nose.

I scrunch *my* nose. Then I pick up the scent of something burning. Belatedly, I remember. "Oh crap. The bacon."

A plume of smoke escapes the oven door when I open it. Irene, a whiz in the kitchen, rushes to the window above the sink and pries it open. I slap the vent fan on.

The bacon is just shy of charred. "Oh, thank goodness."

"I'll eat any kind of bacon, but that was close," Irene says as she picks up a piece, gingerly crunching into it. "Next year, you won't be home to make breakfast like this." Our parents are lunch and dinner cooks. Breakfast on the other hand? Bagels, cereal, oatmeal, and fruit—the kids take our pick. Until Mom taught me how to cook.

"That means you'll have to take my place, Irene."

"You won't mind if I use your apron?"

"No, I won't mind." I look down at the threadbare canvas apron I've used since I was little. It was from the holiday cookie decorating party for Carm's tenth birthday. "Hold that thought," I say, then reach for my phone. Sure enough, after checking the calendar, Carm and I have cookie decorating planned for tomorrow—number seven on our Mission: Holly list.

A notification flies in. A text from Teddy. My breath hitches.

> **Teddy:** What are you doing right now?

> **Lila:** Cooking breakfast

> **Teddy:** Still up to hang out?

> **Lila:** Half hour?

Teddy: Great! Come to the climbing gym

I've got to practice for the competition

Wanna show you why I love it

Lila: Okay.

A mixture of thrill and relief courses through me. That he doesn't think last night was a mistake.

I sure don't.

I press my fingers against my lips, relishing the gentle and sure way he kissed me.

"Ate!"

I look up from my phone as Irene grabs the ladle and flips the pancakes. The bottoms are burned.

"Maybe *I* should take over even before you leave," she quips.

"You know what?" An idea rushes through me. I untie my apron and slip it over her head. "Maybe you're right."

"What are you doing?"

"I've got to go. You finish up. There's only a couple more to make from the batter."

"Oh . . . okay."

I rush to my closet and sort through my hanging clothes. Am I really going to see Teddy for the first time post-kiss in workout gear? What is a spectator supposed to wear at a climbing gym?

Lila: What should I wear

Teddy: Something comfortable

Blue leggings or black leggings?

Short sleeve or long sleeve?

I settle for blue leggings and a short-sleeve T-shirt.

Hair in a braid or a ponytail or a bun? I twist my hair around my hand.

"Where are you going?"

I startle at the question. Irene's leaning against the doorway.

"Is this even my room? And who's watching the stove?" I stall, knowing full well that whatever I say to Irene will be repeated to my mother. I'm not ready to talk about Teddy and me yet, because *I* don't even know what we are. Especially because Ms. Velasco and Mom are such close friends.

"I turned the burner off. So?"

A growl escapes my lips. "I'm going to work out."

Irene frowns. "When have you ever worked out?"

"When I decided that I should start working out. Are you my keeper or something?"

"No, I guess not." She sighs. "Oh. Can I inherit your old laptop now? I have to turn in an assignment, and my Chromebook is acting up again."

"First of all, fastest change of subject of all time. Second, why do you have an assignment due?"

"It's extra credit." She scowls. "I need all the points I can get."

I think through the programs and documents I have up, and whether there's anything important she might come across or delete in the process. "Yes, you can have it early, but I've got to back it up before you can take it permanently."

She nods. "Can I use it while you're out, at least?"

"That's fine."

"Thank you," she says, then stills.

I huff. "What?"

"Where are you working out?"

"At the gym."

"Which gym and do you even have a membership? Do you even know what to do at a gym?"

"Irene!" I throw my hands up, exasperated.

"Geez, Ate, I'm just asking a question. I'm out." She flashes me the peace sign; though, as usual, speaking to my sister has left me without a lick of peace.

I arrive at Climb Holly about a half hour later to a fairly empty parking lot. Inside, music blares, and the gym is a ghost town, with only two climbers on the walls.

"Welcome back," Sarah, the party planner, says. "You're here to meet Teddy, right?"

I nod, warmth flooding my cheeks.

"He took care of your entrance fee. Since you're in the system, you can go on ahead and meet him. Do you need a locker for your backpack? Or shoes?"

Shoes? "Oh no. I'm not climbing today. I'll probably do some reading."

Confusion passes across her face. "All right. Have a good morning. He's on wall number one."

I spot Teddy when I turn the corner. He's standing with two guys, both climbers, already in harnesses and colorful climbing shoes. He's animated as he speaks, hands joining in with his storytelling.

This is Teddy at his happiest. His body is relaxed, and his smile is so contagious that I feel my lips spread out into their own grin.

My grin is so bodacious that I realize, once and for all, that I want *that*. I want to feel that about whatever I do in the future. I want that now.

Carm's words filter back: *Writing is what you do.*

And Teddy's statement last night: *You're so good at it.*

Is writing that?

Then Teddy spots me, and his smile, if possible, widens. It pulls me out of my thoughts.

That smile is for me.

I glide toward him and take his outstretched hand. When he leans down and plants a kiss on my cheek, and introduces me to the other two climbers, Jared and Matt, it's as if I've been dropped into my favorite contemporary romance. His sure grip, the way he includes me in their conversation, and the glances he gives me, as if he and I were always a thing, is so romantic.

I don't fully understand what Teddy's mission is until I'm in front of a wall, and he's holding up a harness.

"Whoa. Wait a second." I step back.

He gestures upward. "This is the beginner wall. All the holds are jugs, which are easy to grab on to and easy to stand on. Wanna try it?"

"Not really."

He laughs. "What were you going to do this whole time? Watch me?"

"Yeah! And read."

He rests a hand on the wall and relaxes his stance. "What's on the reading docket?"

"Holiday by the Lake."

"Back-to-back movie and book. Isn't that redundant?"

"I guess I'm in the mood since . . ." *Since we kissed.*

His cheeks darken in a blush as if reading my thoughts. "How about another negotiation?"

"Okay." I brace myself. "Go ahead."

"What if, in exchange for you climbing this wall, I'll read *Holiday by the Lake.*"

"Now *that* is interesting." Imagining Teddy with *Holiday by the Lake* is as enticing as a hot cocoa bomb. But then I think of something better. "How about a buddy read? Like a book club with the two of us."

He groans, but he says, "For this climb, okay. Fine. What's your shoe size?"

I tell him. And while he jogs off to grab them, I look across to the wall, to these *jugs,* painted red. They are, admittedly, large. My fingers could easily grasp them, and I can envision my toes slipping into them to help prop me up.

My brothers climbed a similar wall the other day.

He returns, and while I change out of my shoes, I say, "I . . . I'm scared."

"Of heights?"

"No. It's just that I've never done this." I stand and move toward him.

"Okay, we can work with that."

"Why do we have to work with that? Why not just leave it??" I think about all the change I've endured in the past month. That, and knowing there's more up ahead, as soon as this winter break ends. What happens when Teddy goes back to school? What will I decide if I'm offered that internship? What if my financial aid package is much less than I'm hoping for?

He shrugs. "I dunno, maybe it's to show yourself that you can do something scary. And maybe taking one small step toward something scary can lead to other things?"

"Like getting hurt?"

My words seem to halt him.

Because trying something new sometimes leads to pain. Doing something hard and scary doesn't always lead to triumph. It happened to my dad and to our family, respectively. And it could happen to us, whenever this is over.

I don't need to learn lessons twice—it's my superpower.

I know I've taken him aback. But he doesn't get angry. Instead, he sets both of his hands on my hips.

"Yeah, sometimes it means you *do* get hurt. Sometimes it means falling. But sometimes it's grabbing that extra bit of air and then catching yourself. What I love about climbing is that there's a little bit of faith on that wall—faith in whatever you might believe in, in stuff that's unexplained, even in the magic of the holidays. But I'm also counting on myself. On my own hands, on my own feet, on my own brain."

I blurt out the question that's been swirling in my mind. "What happens when you leave for school? I know it was just a kiss. It's probably nothing."

His gaze drops. "I don't know."

My mouth quirks. "At least you're honest."

He squeezes my hips gently. "Hey. 'I don't know' means just that. But you didn't let me finish. I want to find out what happens. A kiss isn't just nothing."

"Really?"

"Yeah. I'm not afraid of taking a leap." His eyes gleam. "But how about you? Are you willing to step up?"

I think about how much my dad worked to rebuild his business, about how much Teddy practices at climbing so that he doesn't fall again. At Ms. Velasco, who charged on with the Bookworm Inn after Lola Mae passed away. My mother, who kept our family afloat. I nod.

He leads me to the wall and tells me to touch it. As I do, he gives me instructions—grab and step for all the red holds—and reminds me that he's right there. I listen to him intently. He assists me into my harness, pulls on my straps.

"I've got you," he reminds me. "And, yeah, so much relies on your muscle to get you up there, but in the beginning, especially when you're learning, you've got to lean on the belay too. Trust that someone else will make up for the moments you miss."

He backs up to his position and leaves me alone with the wall. I grab the red jug just above me and press my foot into the bottom one.

Then I hike my left leg so my left toe connects with a red jug and swing my right hand up to grab the nearest one. Fear jolts through me; I'm no longer on the ground. My heart ratchets up to my throat, but as I focus the weight of my fear into my legs and hands, into my fingers and toes, the truth becomes clear.

I'm holding myself up.

I look back down, to Teddy, who smiles up at me. "You're doing great."

I trust him; I'm ready for more. This time, I hike my right leg up, and then my left hand. My heart soars. I do it again. And again.

"All right, Lila, come back down," Teddy yells from below.

"I'm only halfway up."

"I know. But since this is your first time, let's see how you do climbing back down."

"But—" I object; my competitive spirit has kicked in. Now that I'm so close to that bell, I can surely reach it.

"Lila," he calls out sweetly.

I look down, and the realization of how high I am catches up to me. Sweat races down my back.

"One jug at a time, Lila."

I even out my breathing, slowly but surely, and with shaking limbs, climb down the wall. By the time my feet hit the mat, I'm overcome with both relief and joy. When Teddy approaches, I launch myself at him and throw my arms around his neck. "I did it."

"You did," he says into my hair when he sets me down. "You took the leap. You're the bravest person I know."

But later, as I watch Teddy navigate a boulder from the sidelines with adrenaline still running through me and a copy of *Holiday by the Lake* on my lap, an email rings in from BookGalley.

This time, I wonder if I'm brave enough.

Dear Lila,

On behalf of BookGalley, I would like to extend our thanks for applying to our internship program. After careful consideration of all qualified applicants, we are pleased to offer you an interview via video chat. If this still interests you, please respond to this email so we can schedule a time with Martina Flowers, our BookGalley HR director.

Sincerely,
Alexis Lehman
Internship Coordinator
BookGalley

Chapter 23

"So what are you going to do?" The muscles in Carm's forearms flex as she squeezes the clear bag of green icing onto her cookie. We're at Yule Be Baking, the pastry shop on Second Street, set up in a windowed-corner with three other couples for a 2:00 p.m. cookie decorating class.

"I'm not sure. I still have to make the video interview appointment." I look down at my cookie, which is supposed to be my version of a decorated reindeer. Except it is a mess. My piping skills have left too much to be desired, and frankly, my patience is shot. So I decide to take a bite out of the cookie instead and stare out the window.

Downtown Holly is abuzz. While the town is usually busy before Christmas, it's post-Christmas when we see the flood of tourists. Perhaps it's the fact that New Year's Eve signals fun, or that this year, visitors are flocking in early for New Year's Eve by the Lake. Whatever the case, the vibe is joyous.

The cookie is delicious, and I take another bite. "What would you do?"

"About the interview? No question. Do it." She lays down her piping bag and gestures to her cookie. "Look at that perfect layer of icing."

"It *is* perfect."

She scrunches her nose at my disaster cookie. "You're not even trying."

"I don't think my icing's the right consistency, though it is delicious."

"I don't believe you. You're stressed about this internship. Let's talk about your pros and cons again."

I groan. "I've been talking myself through those for the last twenty-four hours." Since I received the email yesterday, I even contemplated broaching my parents for their opinion. But that would entail spilling everything—including my years of being the anonymous blogger behind TnT.

"What's stopping you?" Carm prods.

"Besides my parents? Revealing who I am to the world. That it will be a time commitment I can't juggle right now. It's another job."

"But the internship is paid, right? It would help with Syracuse."

"That's true." I lick my lips. The sugar gives me a boost.

"And is it bad for people to know who you are?" She picks up the piping bag of red icing.

"I . . . I don't know. Honestly, it's been nice to be able to write without anyone knowing who I am. I mean, besides you and Teddy."

"But what about it do you not want people to know?"

"I don't know." I take another bite of cookie.

Carm lifts her gingerbread man that she iced with an ugly red sweater. "Ta-da!"

"It's perfect."

"I started to do a Santa jacket and switched it up."

"Very smart."

"A person's got a right to change their mind, Lila." Her stare is pointed.

"Yes, Mom." I roll my eyes.

"And . . . speaking of . . . maybe it wouldn't be so bad to tell your parents." She wipes her fingers with a napkin. "I mean, after an initial freak-out."

I shiver at the thought, and we both laugh. I relax into the moment despite the solemn turn of the conversation. The music piping through the speakers is a soothing instrumental holiday song. I'm with a friend who's basically family. We're icing cookies while staring onto a pretty sidewalk view. "It hasn't been so bad, our Mission: Holly excursion. Slightly cheesy, but fun."

"Are you feeling the spirit?" She grins.

"I am, thanks to you."

"I'm not sure it's just me who's helping you do that."

"Stop." I pick up the next cookie from the stack. "I'm trying to work here." Though it feels like the sugar has gone straight to my head. After yesterday's climbing session, Teddy and I hung out the rest of the afternoon. Tonight we plan to meet up again, this time with his climbing friends.

"I'll only stop if you quit smiling."

So I suck in my cheeks, which makes us roll with laughter.

"You really like him," she says.

"I do."

"I bet Ms. Velasco and your parents are loving this."

At the mention of our families, I still. "They don't know. And everything's so new with us. The other night was—"

"The other night? This calls for extra cookies to make. Or eat. Because I want to know *everything*. Wait here." She heads to the counter to purchase more plain sugar cookies.

My cheeks burn with my leftover glee.

"That was vicious. My quads are killing me," Jared says.

"Your quads? My lats," Matt counters. "How's your ankle, Teddy?"

I look at Teddy, mid sip of my iced tea. We're at Poinsettia's Pizza, snug in a booth. All around us are locals huddled around pies lifted up on stands. Only bits of cheese are left on our raised silver platters; two pies gone in fifteen minutes.

His ankle?

I can't make out Teddy's expression in the glare of the canned lights hanging from the ceiling. He didn't mention an injury, despite the dozens of texts we exchanged today, mostly about *Holiday by the Lake,* which he started reading after our climbing session. When I walked into Poinsettia's an hour ago, Teddy and his friends were already seated.

"It's fine," he says.

Except there's a hitch to his tone.

"What happened?" I ask.

"I was bouldering. Just let go too quickly and twisted it when I landed. It isn't a big deal."

Jared snorts. "It sure was. I was clear across the gym and heard you yell after you flopped." He claps his hands together for effect, and the couple in the booth behind him turns. Jared and Matt laugh, and Teddy snickers.

"I've got a brace on." He shifts and directs my attention under the table, to a brace wrapped around his ankle. "I hurt it before, so I'm used to putting this on whenever I have to."

"Not your head, though?"

"Nope." His eyes flash a warning, and it takes me aback.

While the group moves on in the conversation, a leftover weird vibe runs between us; even as we pay and the other two head out, Teddy and I are left in an awkward silence.

After a beat, he speaks up. "You know, when I talked about my concussion, that was meant to be a secret."

"I . . . I'm sorry. I was just concerned."

"I get it." He reaches out to take my hand and squeezes it. "But I didn't tell you all that so you would worry about me. It's why I picked a college that's far enough away from my parents, and why I haven't told Tita Lou. I want to be able to decide if I'm okay. I don't want to be held back."

One of the things about reading and blogging about so many books is that I've learned that everything has to be placed into context. Right now, in this context, I understand exactly what Teddy is saying, and yet, the words—*I don't want to be held back*—land between us with an unavoidable thud.

Is this just about his secret? Or is it about us as a couple?

"Okay," is all I can say.

He heaves a breath. "She's going to see my brace."

I still. "She?"

"Tita Lou. She's going to ask what happened. And I . . . I don't know what I'm going to say."

"Where does she think you are?"

"Out." His lips flatten into a line. "I don't give her much information."

"Then let her know that you were with me." I smile.

"No, I don't want to bring you into—"

I shake my head. "Just say we were sledding down Wonderhill. If she asks me about it tomorrow at work, I'll cover for you."

"Really?"

I nod. "Yes."

"Thank you, thank you, thank you." He brings my hand to his lips and kisses it. My worries from a few seconds ago dissipate. "With the New Year's Eve event, things are more tense than usual. I do plan to tell her about the competition, maybe after New Year's Eve. And about us, if that's okay with you."

"I . . ." It's official, I have become the ice that's melting in my iced tea. "It's totally okay with me."

"Good. Because I hate all of these secrets. And I just need a little more time, to strategize telling Tita Lou and my parents, about my climbing, and even this ankle. I hate being a liar and a hypocrite. But I also want to do this competition. My conscience, though . . . it's killing me." He rubs my knuckle with his thumb. "Being with you, and seeing how you are with your friends and family . . . I miss that. I miss having people who care about what I'm doing. And I realized it's not because they don't care, but it's because I don't let them in. I'm trying to be better. I'm trying to find my way through this."

"I know, Teddy." I snuggle into him to show him my support, and he wraps an arm around my shoulder. He kisses me sweetly, but even the press of his lips doesn't take away my own guilt.

Because I'm in the exact same boat.

What am I going to do about *my* secrets?

Chapter 24

Finally, New Year's Eve at the Lake is here! On my mother's calendar, the date is circled in red, and Mom and I picked out our outfits yesterday. We got ready at 8:00 p.m., and now, at 10:00 p.m., our minivan rolls up Bookworm Drive after security checks our tickets partway up.

The driveway is lit by the red lights of the vehicles waiting their turn, and when we enter the parking lot, Chief Dasher welcomes each vehicle. Mom rolls down the window. "Hey, Chief!"

"Hi, Cat. There's ample parking in the back, and you can go in the employee entrance since you have Lila with you."

"Thank you!" Mom says, bypassing the cars weaseling their way through the small spaces and parking farther down. We touch up our makeup and grab our *Holiday by the Lake* books and our phones (I check twice to make sure I have the right one) before jumping out.

Music blares from inside the Inn. Still, it can't compete with the pounding of my heart. Jonah Johanson. Remy Castillo. Teddy

Rivera. All in one place. Add it to my looming decision about the internship interview, and it's like all of my emotions are bursting out at once.

We walk through the employee entrance, and the passageway from the Inn to the gift shop teems with employees. Everyone is on their own trajectory, carrying product or speaking into walkie-talkies. And when we enter the gift shop, it is a whole other level of loud.

Mom grabs a flyer from KC, who tackles me with a hug before being pulled away, and eyes her watch. "Looks like everyone is hanging around here until the panel, which is in about ten minutes. And fireworks at midnight, then the book signing." She presses the flyer against her chest with dramatic flair and breathes, "I can't believe we're going to meet Remy."

I hug her, she's so cute.

We're interrupted by Mrs. Bruno, a nurse and one of Mom's coworkers. As they start chatting, it's the perfect time for me to escape. "I'm going to walk around to see who's here."

"Okay, Iha . . ." Her attention drifts back to Mrs. Bruno mid-sentence. Hence the reason why, when we attend parties, we have to give Mom a thirty-minute heads-up before our exit because her farewells are so lengthy. There's always last-minute juicy gossip.

I'm sweating by the time I make my way to my library, where people are milling about looking at the spines. I feel a tug against my arm. It's Teddy, dressed in his Bookworm Inn uniform. He gestures to the back, and with a final look at Mom, who has joined a circle with other Holly General staff, I follow him down toward the break room. He pulls me in, shuts the door, and locks it.

I burst into a giggle, then wrap my arms around his neck.

When he stares down at me with his brown eyes, arms

encircling my waist, everything is perfect. I drink in both him and this moment. It's already the best New Year's Eve ever, and the festivities haven't even started yet. And though it's only been a day since we've seen each other, and only a half hour since our last text, it feels like too much time has passed. "How is it out there?" I ask.

"Worse than that last night we worked together. So busy that no one can see the arrows on the ground. At one point, the line wrapped around the back of the store. And someone started humming the theme song and everyone joined in. It's a whole other level of fandom."

I laugh. "Well, I know something that might make you feel better."

"Yes. Anything, please."

I get on my tiptoes and kiss him. I mean for it to be chaste and silly. But he tastes like chocolate, and I go in for another kiss, and another one. His hands grip my waist, and I pull him down to me, because I can't get enough of his lips on mine.

I hear the sound of jingle bells but I push it away. Then a second set of jingle bells chime, and Teddy looks up and turns his head toward the door. As we break contact, I slacken.

"It's almost time for the panel. I'm assigned to help manage the crowd. You shouldn't be late." He grins, then kisses me on the nose. "Meet me at the pier afterward?"

"Okay."

"I'll walk out first. Give it a couple of seconds before you do." He opens the door; then with a wink, he shoots down the hallway.

I'm not sure that even the panel can top that.

I have stars in my eyes throughout the panel event. Despite sitting too far away, I'm swept up watching these two beloved actors recount their experience working on the film. Mom and I hold hands the whole time when she's not taking pictures—we're both that amped and excited.

Jonah Johanson is not such a heartthrob in real life—Teddy's right, he's more like a dad—but he's still charming and can elicit a giggle from the crowd. He knows how to work it.

But Remy Castillo is a star. Her presence is commanding, and in a weird way, she reminds me of Mom—no-nonsense but quick to laughter.

After the panel, Mom hangs by the exit, showing me the fangirl, or perhaps the stalker, she really is. A few minutes later, Ms. Velasco exits with Kira. And . . .

Holy Heat Miser. It's *them.*

"That was absolutely fantastic," says Jonah Johanson. The timbre of his voice sends fangirl shivers up my spine. I take it back—up close, I can see Leo. He exudes confidence. With his salt-and-pepper hair and both hands hiked up on his hips, he brings me right back to the film, to the moment where his younger self stands up to a bully who happened to be picking on the younger Estelle.

And next to him is Remy herself.

Standing an inch or two taller than me, the connection is instant—er, at least on my end. And while wrinkles crinkle the sides of her eyes and mouth, she's just as pretty. Jonah pales next to Remy. It's already a once-in-a-lifetime moment, meeting a film star, and the fact that she's one of only a handful of Filipino American actors on the big screen is overwhelming.

It's like you don't know what you're missing until you get it.

"Oh, this is perfect," Ms. Velasco says. "Remy and Jonah, this is my best friend Cat and her daughter Lila. Ladies, unfortunately we can't hang out for too long. It's time for a quick break for them before the countdown and fireworks."

My super fangirl status emerges in what surely looks like a manic grin. And yet, the only thing that leaves my mouth is, "Hi."

Apparently I've lost the ability to form words, because when Remy says something indiscernible—I only know that her lips are moving and what is that shade of red because it's perfect for her skin, never mind I don't wear red lipstick—I answer with, "Uh-huh."

There's a little more small talk between Mom, Ms. Velasco, Kira, and the actors, but my brain descends into a fog.

"This was so much fun," Mom says to me after Ms. Velasco leads the stars to their break room. "I'm going to be on cloud nine for days. To have them here makes the movie come alive."

Teddy comes to mind. He's going to freak when I tell him what just happened. "Mom, I have some friends I want to say hi to. Can I—"

"Oh, no worries, Iha. Go see them while I grab a drink and catch up with Lou. I'll look for you closer to midnight."

It takes what feels like a herculean effort to weave through the crowd, and the chilly air outside is sweet relief. I shoot a quick text to Carm: *I met them!*

Carm isn't a fan of *Holiday by the Lake,* but she sends me three rows of random emojis and exclamation points.

Then I take the short, de-iced path to the pier. Teddy is already there.

And he's laughing at me.

"What?"

"You've got this wild look on your face. You must have met them."

"I did!" I do a little dance, right into his arms, and breathe him in. Somehow, I'm not a bit cold. "It was amazing." I squeal one more time, and he laughs.

"Hey, so . . . I got you a present." The rumble of his voice against my skin makes me tremble.

A present?

"But I don't have a present for you," I manage to say.

"I didn't do it so we'd have a gift exchange," he whispers. "After you climbed the other day, I just thought . . . It's something small." He straightens and pulls a wrapped rectangular box from his back pocket.

"Thank you." I accept the gift, then peel the wrapping paper off, revealing a craft box. I open it to find a thin, light brown leather bookmark with a tassel. On one side, embossed, is my name. "Oh, Teddy."

"Do you like it?"

"I do. It's so pretty." I run a finger over the embossed area, the letters distinct. "Is this from—"

"Holly Paperie. But the embossing was done by Blizzard Bags. They were nice enough to do it for me last minute. It's to say thank you, for listening. It means a lot to me."

The thought and care—it's overwhelming. So I just squeeze him tight against me. "You got me that one time, so it only makes sense that I've got you too."

"Belay," he whispers, understanding my reference. He lifts my chin with a finger, and with a heartfelt expression, kisses me. "Happy New Year. And guess what?"

I'm basking in this moment, in what will become one of the most memorable nights of my life. "What?"

"We're currently doing the number one thing on the Mission: Holly list."

Kiss on the Bookworm Inn Pier. "Oh my God. You're right!"

He peers at me. "Think Carm will be pissed?"

"Nope. I bet she wants to experience this one with someone else."

We fall into silence, and it's as if he's run out of steam. I study his face and realize he looks exhausted. "You okay?"

"Not really . . . I just got off the phone with my parents. It was supposed to be a simple New Year's Eve phone call that turned into them harping on me about school. They gave me a guilt trip for not spending the holiday with them. And I guess they checked my registration at Syracuse, and they know . . ."

"Oh, shoot."

"Yeah . . . I'm deep in it."

"Did you tell them about your competition in a few days?"

He shakes his head. "I didn't. I wanted to tell Tita Lou first, which I was going to do today. But I didn't gauge how busy it was going to be around here."

"You can tell her after the fireworks. It's a good way to start the new year."

He nods solemnly. "How about you? Have you decided what to do about the internship?"

I shake my head.

"Did you respond back to schedule the interview?"

"No." I look away. "I know, I know. What's an interview? But it feels so big. What's the point of going through with the interview if I'm not going to do it at all?"

He catches my gaze. His hands rest gently on my shoulders. "It's okay to be scared."

"It's not fear. It's uncertainty."

But as I say the words, I wonder. Am I scared? And why? This isn't like climbing up a wall. There's no risk of falling or getting a concussion. But somehow the potential for getting hurt still feels real.

"I'll figure things out. Soon. But tonight," I remind him, resting my hands on his chest. He pulls me closer to him. "Tonight, we celebrate."

"All right." He presses a kiss on my nose, then inhales deeply. "Lila, I also have to tell you something."

There's a crack in his voice, and I look up to his troubled expression. "Hmm?"

"Teddy? Lila?" A woman's voice interrupts us, and we look up to Ms. Velasco approaching us, with Mom at her side. "I wanted us to be together for the fireworks. But I guess the two of you got the memo already."

And while Ms. Velasco is grinning, Mom is not. Her expression is stone-cold.

Teddy steps back, but we keep our hands clasped.

"Lila. What are you doing?" Mom's interrogative gaze slides from me to Ms. Velasco. "Did you know about this?"

"I had no idea." At Mom's silence, Ms. Velasco frowns. "Don't worry, I'm sure it's not serious."

Whoa. Teddy and I aren't serious, but hearing it like that takes me aback.

"I hope not," Mom replies. "Teddy's . . . well . . . and Lila . . ."

Ms. Velasco half laughs. "What about Teddy?"

"First of all, he's in college. And second, he's everywhere."

"Everywhere?" Teddy asks, eyebrows plunging in concern.

"Now, Cat, you're out of line," Ms. Velasco warns.

"You said so yourself, Lou. You can't keep him in check. You don't know where he is half the time, and Lila . . . she's in high school."

"Hello?" I lift a hand. "We're right here."

"I'll have you know that Teddy's the one who's been encouraging her to apply for that internship."

"What internship?" Mom frowns.

"Mom." I raise my voice, though I'm looking at Teddy with one question running through my head: How does Ms. Velasco know about the internship?

"For that book review site," Ms. Velasco continues. "I had no idea she had this amazing blog. I took a read myself, and I'm so impressed. Tinsel and Tropes. How clever."

"Tita Lou," Teddy jumps in, at the same time my mother turns to me incredulously. Teddy continues. "Lila, that's what I wanted to tell you. I'm Santa with a View."

I reel back. "Santa with a View? You sent me the link?"

"I did."

"Why didn't you say so?" This is all too much at once.

"It was before we were . . . and I thought you wouldn't have applied if you knew that I was the one who sent it."

I shake my head. "I don't even care about that. What I can't believe is that you told her," I whisper.

"I . . . It just came out," he says.

"Lila?" Mom asks.

I glance up at Ms. Velasco, then at Teddy, and then at my mother, whose confusion is evident on her face. Anger and disappointment swirl inside me. It rises up like the drift during a snowstorm, just as someone announces the five-minute count-down to midnight.

My mother excuses herself from our circle. At her departure, anger wins out. I kept my side of the bargain. Teddy didn't.

"If you're spilling my secrets, then maybe you should spill yours too, Teddy," I say. "You should ask him about where else he's been spending his time, Ms. Velasco."

I pull my hand from Teddy's grasp and take off after my mom.

Chapter 25

SATURDAY, JANUARY 1

I spend the first minute of the new year in our minivan with my mother, with fireworks lighting up the sky behind us, the popping noises resonating in the space even though the windows are rolled up tight. But it doesn't drown out the somber mood. My teeth are still chattering, more from nervousness rather than the chill.

After the fireworks, Mom finally speaks. "What's that about, Lila? What does she mean, blog?"

"It's a book blog."

"Okay?" She crosses her arms.

So I explain. I go back to the beginning, when I started it, how it's almost two years old, that it's something I truly enjoy. I explain Teddy's role in the internship, and how I both do and don't want a chance at it.

I know I'm in trouble because of the silence. My mother is usually *anything* but speechless.

She stares out the front windshield. "Why did you keep it a secret from us?"

"Because I knew you would react this way. You don't like social media at all, and I knew you and Dad wouldn't understand."

"And yet you did it anyway."

"I did. I love my blog, Mom."

Mom sighs. "Do you know what's sad about all of this? I didn't get to share this love with you. You made so many assumptions, Lila. You thought that Dad and I wouldn't change our minds. You thought that we couldn't be bothered with what you love. You thought that we wouldn't be sensitive to what you needed. All this time, I thought bio was what you loved. Are you changing your mind there too? Is writing what you want to do?"

"Is that such a bad thing?"

"That's not it. But I don't know what's going on here, Lila. I feel like I'm suddenly looking at a different person."

I cringe. "You don't mean that."

"I do—because of everything you've said thus far. What am I supposed to do with that? And this thing with Teddy. What is that?"

"That thing with Teddy is—was—new. And sweet. And I like him."

"I don't know what to believe."

I feel my temper rising, and suddenly I can't shove it down any longer. "You assume things about me too. You assume that I know exactly what I want. You assume that I will always rise to whatever expectations you've set for me. You assume that things are going fine, when maybe I want different. When I have been confused about choosing between something I really love and something I know will be practical. When I've been worried about doing enough so I don't burden you and Dad. Why do you think I'm trying to pick up so many hours? I want to do the right thing, but sometimes I don't know what that is. So it's not just me who assumes. It's you too."

My mother's eyes glass over, but she blinks away her tears in the next second. She opens her mouth to say one more thing, then stops herself. Instead she starts the car, and we head home.

Chapter 26

For the second night in a row, I toss and turn. And when I finally decide to get up, I check my phone, Teddy's texts fill my screen, with various versions of *I'm sorry.* I'm sorry, too, but I'm still filled with anger and regret. And I don't know what to do about it.

What a mess. My heart hurts from my conversation with Mom, and the conversation that Teddy and I aren't having.

If the first day of the new year was an indication of how the rest of the year is going to go, then I might as well phone it in now.

I groan, covering my face with a pillow.

The sound of a creaking door takes me out of my head. I peek to the side of my pillow and see Irene's face, contorted in worry. She has my old laptop open. "Ate Lila?"

"Yes." My voice croaks.

"You okay?"

"No."

Her eyes round into saucers. "This is a first."

I groan again. It's bad enough to have disappointed my mom,

but now I'm failing my sister too. I have a reputation to protect. Ates are supposed to be indestructible, and here I am, falling apart. "Let me give you some advice, Irene. There's no such thing as secrets. Because they always reveal themselves."

"Oh." She bites her bottom lip, and she goes silent.

It's curious.

"What. What 'oh'?" I finally ask.

"Oh, then I might as well tell you that I looked through your emails. The notifications kept popping up, you know?"

I slide the pillow off my face and push away the strands of hair that imprinted themselves on my cheeks. "You read my emails."

"And everything. Tinsel and Tropes. It's *so* good."

I should be horrified, but I can't muster the energy. Instead, I smile. "Yeah?"

"And I think you should get dressed. From the top up, anyway."

"Why?"

"Well . . . I kinda made an appointment for your interview."

I sit up. "You what?"

"You wouldn't email them back, and the lady sounded so convincing. Today was the last day. Anyway, it was really easy. I just clicked on the link that took me to their calendar and I put your name in. So"—she glances at the laptop clock—"you have, like, seventeen minutes."

"Irene." I press my fingers against the bridge of my nose. "Are you telling me—"

"That I'm way more observant than you think? I'm an ate too, you know." She pulls me out of bed. "Now you have sixteen minutes. And I have the most perfect outfit for you."

Sometimes it takes a snowstorm to bring two people together, but sometimes it takes one person—and someone you least expect—to help save the day.

The face looking back at me from my dresser mirror is a little more put together than how I actually feel inside. Mirror Lila has her hair combed and braided down one shoulder. Her cheeks are pink from blush, eyes lined with liner. Her lips shimmer with a red gloss that's supposed to show up well on video chat.

Or, Irene says so anyway.

From behind me, and looking straight at my reflection, she says, "Whatcha think?"

And honestly if I didn't have makeup on, I would have cried. Because I needed this. "Thank you."

"Eh." She shrugs, like it's nothing. "So, you've literally got three minutes." She's scrambling around me. She fluffs my blankets straight, lines up the pillows, then brings my laptop to my desk. Then, changing her mind, she stacks four of my books and then props the laptop on top of it. "Is that high enough? You need good angles and light."

I don't know what to say. So, I do the thing that requires the least bit of verbal effort. I wrap my arms around her. She stiffens at first, then melts into me. After beats of silence, she says, "I'm still going to repaint your room."

I croak out a laugh; her comedic timing is perfect. "You have my blessing."

From her pocket her phone buzzes. Her eyebrows lift. "You'd better log on."

"Was that an alarm?"

"'Course." She slips her phone out and presses the snooze button. "I learned from the best."

I snicker. "Not sure who you're talking about. I don't even know what I'm doing."

"Aw, Ate. I don't think anyone knows what they're doing, but I think you might know what the next step is." She has a faint and encouraging smile on her face. "You just have to admit it." She turns me toward the screen. Then she backs out of my room with a final wave. "Kick butt."

I nod, still with my sister's words hanging in the air: *You just have to admit it.*

No more secrets. It's time.

TINSEL AND TROPES
A HOLIDAY BOOK BLOG

Title: Holiday by the Lake by Charlene Dizon
GENRE/CATEGORY: CONTEMPORARY FICTION

It's our second anniversary! Look below this post for a surprise!

How does one make a true apology?

This is a reread of *Holiday by the Lake*, which I first read about five years ago. I don't do very many rereads, because there are so many new books on my list to tackle. But this season begged for a second chance.

The first time I read it, I focused on the romance and the gorgeous setting. I remember being swept up by the author's descriptions of the town and its people. But this time, what jumped out at me was how the characters interacted—how they fought and apologized. At how real and sincere they were when they did so. Not to spoil it, but these characters were tough on each other, both in the past and in the present, and I wondered—would that friendship have held up in real life?

In a lifetime, a person can have a spectrum of friendships. Some lifelong, and others, not so much. Some remain lighthearted throughout, and some run deep from the jump. There are the friendships you make by choice, and some made by happenstance. Many of these friendships tend to fizzle out. Even though it's a romance, *Holiday by the Lake* is about two people who have to decide if all their struggles are worth their friendship.

In all ways, it's about a second-chance relationship, my most favorite trope!

Do I recommend this book the second time around? Absolutely. Not only does it have a happily-ever-after—and was adapted into one of the best movies of all time—but it's a reminder that we have to try to apologize when we do something wrong.

Pros: Twin timelines are so fun! Just when you have a question about what happened in the past, it jumps backward in time.

Cons: If you watched the movie first, then it will be hard to separate the movie from the book.

Recommended for: Everyone
Rating: 5 stars
***

Happy second anniversary to us! Tinsel and Tropes started with me wanting to spread the word about books I love. I decided that my identity would be anonymous because I wanted to protect my and my family's privacy. Over time, I liked the fact that this blog was less about me and more about the books I read.

But here's the thing: If you read the posts carefully, this blog really is most definitely about me. In the last two years, this has been like my diary, even if I hadn't realized it at the time.

So, my name is Lila. I'm the book blogger behind Tinsel and Tropes. While I won't get much more personal than that, I am ready to admit that this blog means so much to me, and I no longer want to keep it a secret. And I want to celebrate it by giving away a special holiday book box to one reader! Below is a pic—feast your eyes on these five-star reads!

To enter, please leave me a message with the title of your favorite holiday book! I'll announce the winner January 4th at 5pm EST. International okay.

Thank you, loyal readers, for hanging in there, and for reading this blog even if I didn't give it the credit—or give *myself* the credit—that it deserves.

Chapter 27

The long hand on the grandfather clock clicks to the twelve, and the bell chimes nine times.

I pace and cross my arms over my chest. And despite the crackling fireplace and the warm sweater I'm wearing, I'm feeling cold and unsettled.

Yesterday ended better than it started. Martina Flowers from BookGalley was cheerful and encouraging, and we talked about Holly and my blog, and what I wanted to get out of the internship.

I love books, and I want to know if I can do something with that, I said.

And: *Yes, I think I'm now ready to go public as the Tinsel and Tropes author.*

Then, after my half-hour-long interview, I hid back in my bedroom and finished *Holiday by the Lake* and untangled all my thoughts on my blog.

No more secrets.

But right now, my mind's not on that.

Teddy's competition starts in one hour.

I can picture his face, etched in worry. And I wonder who will be there in the crowd to watch him. Did he tell Ms. Velasco about the competition? Did he and his parents make up?

I've got you too.

I meant those words, and it feels wrong for me to be here, at home, instead of there, cheering him on. Even at our family's lowest point, when we thought Dad's business might be gone forever, when they were living in fear from the doxing, I knew, no matter what, my family was there for one another. It's why these last couple of days have been so hard—being at odds with my parents makes me feel like I've lost a part of myself.

My phone buzzes, and I fumble it out of my pocket. Among the dozens of comment notifications from Tinsel and Tropes left by supportive and encouraging readers, there's an email from BookGalley. Yesterday, Martina informed me that status updates would be emailed soon, though I didn't expect it this early.

"'Dear Lila,'" I read aloud. "'Thank you for your application. After consideration, you will advance to the next round of interviews.'"

I clutch the phone against my chest. *I made the next round.*

My first inclination is to text Teddy. But I know we can't fix things over text. Because I need to apologize too. I need to own up to my part.

But there are two other people who I need to tell ASAP.

So I make a pot of coffee while running through the facts in my head. With the phone in my back pocket, I enter my parents' room with two steaming cups, where Mom is perched on the bed and Dad is walking out of their en suite bath. I set the coffee down at each of my parent's side tables.

Then I sit down at the foot of the bed, and I hand Mom my phone.

She stares at it for a beat. Then her eyes get big.

"I made it to the second round. And seeing it, that I made it even this far? It makes me want it more. I want to do this internship, Mom. But even if I don't get it, I think I can write. I take it back—I *know* I can write. Not just blog posts, but maybe other things. Maybe essays, maybe short stories, maybe books. It doesn't mean premed is over and done with, but maybe I can do something in addition to it? I don't know. I haven't figured it out. But I hope you can support me."

My mom is silent, but she reaches for her cup. Then she looks up at me through her lashes, eyes shiny. Tears dot her cheeks.

My mother never cries. She's hard as nails.

This spurs me into my prepared speech, except my feelings flow out instead. "I know I lied. I'm sorry I lied. I get you're mad, and if the tables were turned, I would be too. But please know I won't keep something like this from you ever again." I take a deep breath. "I knew that going public with the blog would change everything, and it has. But I'm still so proud of it. Writing makes me happy."

The silence that follows feels like it lasts forever.

"I'm so proud of you." Mom's voice breaks at the end of her sentence.

Her words bring me to tears. "Still?"

"Still? *Always.* Because of who you are: conscientious, thoughtful, sympathetic, empathetic. I'm not mad. I'm sorry I wasn't there for you when you needed me, that I took you for granted. I should have checked in with you more, and asked, and listened. Those blog posts. They said so much, and they were just . . . lovely."

"You read them?"

"Every single one. And I don't want to miss a single post again. I want to be the first to read everything you write. I want to be here whenever you need me too."

Dad reaches over and clutches Mom's hand. "Iha, we're private, but we have reasons for that."

"Dad."

"No, let me say what I need to say." He holds up a hand. "And even though we had our struggles, I don't want you to live in fear, or in doubt. We want for you to have the life you want, to study the things you love, and to be the person who you need to be. And . . . we don't want you to think it's your job alone to get you where you want to go."

Mom reaches for my hand. "You are not a burden. Your dreams aren't burdens either. Dad and I want the honor of figuring this out together, with you. So whenever your financial package posts, whenever it's time to move you into school, we'll be with you at every step. So congratulations, Lila. BookGalley would be so lucky to have you." Mom sets her cup back on her side table and leans in to hug me. Her embrace is solid and comforting, and I sniff into her shoulder until my heartbeat calms. "I hate to cut this short, Iha, but don't you think we have to go?"

"Go?" I back away. It's then I realize that both my parents are not in their pajamas, but in jeans. Dad's wearing a fleece sweater and is grinning ear to ear. "You mean Teddy's competition?"

"Of course." She stands. "Lou called us last night and invited us. And we always show up for family."

"He did prove himself at karaoke," Dad adds.

Have I already said that my parents are supportive and that Ms. Velasco is the best, ever?

I check my watch. Only forty minutes until his competition begins. "Let's go."

With fifteen minutes left—it's like herding cats to get the whole family moving in one direction—we hurtle into the Climb Holly parking lot. There's no free parking spaces, so Dad swings by the front and I jump out with the twins and Irene. We trudge through the wet snow and fly into the building through the metal double doors. The music is concert-loud, but my focus is solely on finding Teddy. My gaze flits over the people near the boulders, at the competitors idling on the mat.

"I don't see him, Ate." Grant jumps to try to get a better look.

"Climb on my back, Grant," Graham says.

"Do you want me to sneak up front?" Irene offers.

Where is he?

The drive here, as short as it was, felt like it took longer than 364 days to next Christmas. I should have been in this gym already. I should already be in the first row. I should have taken his call two days ago and found a way to have our hard conversation before this competition, so he would know that—

"Lila?"

My gaze slides to the direction of the voice in front of me.

Teddy emerges from the crowd, wearing a tank and shorts. His hair is slicked back, and there's an unreadable expression on his face.

"Teddy." My body moves toward him; my first instinct is to throw my arms around him, but I stop short. "I . . . Good luck today."

"I'm glad you came." Finally, thankfully, he smiles.

It's all the permission I need, and I wrap my arms around his torso. "Teddy, I'm sorry. I shouldn't have told your aunt. I was mad, and shocked—"

"No, it's me who needs to say sorry. I should have never told Tita Lou about your blog. I was trying to cover up my own secrets, and I rambled on and accidentally let your secret slip instead. But I'm done with secrets. Not between us, not with my aunt or with my parents."

"Same. Same times a million." My face aches from smiling so hard.

His hands rest against the nape of my neck, and his expression changes to one of relief. "You're really here."

"I promised I would be."

His voice lowers. "I read your blog post this morning. It was so . . . great. I really like you, Lila. I'm in awe of you. I know we have a lot to talk about. I finished *Holiday by the Lake,* and what you said about friendship and apologies and forgiveness, it was all so honest. Can we try this again?"

"Do we have to go through the whole train Teddy phase?"

"No, though I wouldn't mind reliving the first thing on the Mission: Holly list."

I soak him and this whole moment in. "Who needs a pier anyway?"

"I don't." Teddy lifts my chin with a finger and presses a kiss to my lips. Irene clucks and my brothers croon. But I don't have time to be embarrassed, because I'm too wrapped up in him.

An announcement filters through the speakers, and it catches Teddy's attention. "I have to head up."

"Okay, but one more thing. I made it to the second round for the internship selection."

His face brightens, like the clear blue sky after a snowstorm. "No way."

"Way!"

He hugs and twirls me, until his friends pull him away. It's chaos, but he yells back, "There might be some seats up front. Call for me, so I know where you are."

"You've got it. Good luck!"

A beat later, he's off toward the mat, where he disappears into the crowd.

It takes cajoling and pleading to squeeze myself and my family through the crowd, but we finally find seats close enough to Teddy. He's dusting his hands with chalk as he waits his turn.

At the moment, there's someone else on the boulder, a guy in a red tank. He crawls up the yellow footholds. He extends arms and legs and grips and grunts. Then he pauses with his left hand and left foot in holds. He reaches toward a seemingly out-of-reach hold above him.

His fans cheer and encourage him as he attempts the move. But Red Tank falls short, landing on his feet, and the crowd groans in disappointment.

On the sidelines, Teddy is shaking out his ankle. His expression is serious. I push down all my worry, and instead find my voice.

"Teddy!" I yell.

He doesn't turn. He's looking in the other direction, toward someone else calling his name. When I scan the crowd, I find Ms. Velasco waving, and next to her is a man and a woman. I drag my gaze back to Teddy, who's waving back.

Teddy's parents. They have to be.

When he faces the boulder once more, I try his name again.

This time, he turns in my direction.

"Right here!" I yell.

He finds me in the crowd, expression grim. I know that he's thinking about that reach, that switch in hold. I think of the moments when he's encouraged me. And the one thing he said when I climbed up a wall the first time. I round my hand over my mouth and yell, "I've got you!"

Teddy grins. His smile is so big, it spans ear to ear.

Finally, he's called to the boulder. A beep sounds, and a timer begins. I watch him as he maneuvers the climb with precision. His muscles contort with every move. Next to me, my siblings are screaming, directing, cheering. Dad's clapping. Mom covers her eyes with a hand.

Teddy arrives at the final hold before he has to catch air. I keep my eyes on him. I can't blink.

With my hands covering my mouth in a silent wish, I watch Teddy reach for that hold, and he makes it.

Epilogue

On the twelfth day of Christmas, my true love gave to me: tickets to Wonderhill!

"I can't believe we're doing this." I grumble and creep to the edge of the snow hill. In full snow gear, I peer over. KC and Seb just made it to the bottom of their run—they're cracking up trying to climb out of their snow tube. Carm is at the bottom of our run, standing next to Aiden. She's waving, as if that's going to encourage me to get on this thing faster.

Teddy hefts the two-person snow tube, and it slams against the snow. "This is going to be epic."

"What if I just turn around and go back down the stairs? No one will know any better. See?" I point; the four are dragging their snow tubes back to the waiting area.

"I mean, you can do that, but then you'll miss out on the last thing on your Mission: Holly list."

"I can live with that."

His eyebrows lift, and he gives me a knowing look.

I huff out a breath. "No, no, I can't."

Teddy offers a hand, and I take it. Though there are layers of fabric between our palms and fingers, I still feel his warmth.

Teddy leaves Holly tomorrow. Though he's not due back in Syracuse until mid-January, he'll spend his last week of break in California. Now, armed with a third-place medal from his competition, his next challenge is making peace with his parents. They actually flew in to the Finger Lakes after their phone call on New Year's Eve, and even though Ms. Velasco and the Riveras still have a lot of stuff to work through, I know they're going to be all right.

But I'm not worried about us. Syracuse is a short drive from Holly. And I have my own stuff to figure out in the meantime. Like the internship, which hasn't been announced yet (even though I'm keeping my fingers crossed!), and my major, which I think I'm going to switch to undeclared. We're still waiting on my financial aid offer (any day now, the school said), but I did sit down with Mom and Dad to work out the cost of my academic year with my merit-based scholarship and the college fund they saved for me. That alone lifted the pressure off my shoulders—they're on my side, and whatever happens, they've got me too.

Teddy and I—we're just taking things step by step. Yesterday, we discussed *Holiday by the Lake*, two-person-book-club style, over hot chocolate and chess.

Right now, our next step is going down this hill.

Teddy is already seated in the tube, arms held high. "C'mon, Lila, don't leave me hanging."

I inhale and climb in between his legs. Closer to the ground, Wonderhill is more ominous. Steeper. A shiver runs up my spine—like climbing, this loss of control is frightening—but as if he detects my fear, Teddy wraps his arms around me. In his hold, I relax, because I trust him.

"Lean back when we start going down. I've got you."

I nod. And when we push off down the hill, with the wind against my face, I only feel thrill, and freedom, and hope.

All it took was one little holiday switch.

Acknowledgments

The joy I felt writing this book can only be surpassed by the gratitude I have for the people who helped me achieve this dream. Rachel Brooks—who never, ever ceases in her support, and in this unyielding effort connected me with Wendy Loggia and Hannah Hill. Wendy, thank you for seeing to the heart of me, and, Hannah, thank you for your remarkable editorial direction. You got to Lila's story and her romance with Teddy. You carried that same vision for Holly and the Bookworm Inn. And you had that holiday spirit that transcended edits through the rest of the year.

To the absolute amazing Underlined imprint—thank you! The oh-so-talented Jacqueline Li and Casey Moses for the most adorable cover in the whole entire universe. Kristin Dwyer of LeoPR, my dearest friend and publicist—how *lucky* I am to have shared all these books with you. You are truly the best. To early readers Stephanie Winkelhake and Laura Brown—you are saints, I tell you! Absolute saints! To my #girlswritenight sweethearts: Annie Rains, Rachel Lacey, April Hunt, and Jeanette Escudero. #batsignal Tracey Livesay, Mia Sosa, Priscilla Oliveras, Michele Arris, and Nina Crespo. #5amwritersclub. Tall Poppy Writers.

To my parents, who made Christmas so special for us, no matter the circumstance. To my Greg, who tolerates the extended period of time our decorations are up because inside he knows he loves it all too. And my Fab Four: Greggy, Cooper, Ella, and Anna, whose utmost belief in me is the engine to all my efforts. And finally, to readers, bloggers, reviewers, and booksellers! Thank you for following me here! I couldn't have done any of this without you!

About the Author

Tif Marcelo is a veteran US Army nurse and holds a BS in nursing and a master's in public administration. She believes in and writes about the strength of families, the endurance of friendship, and heartfelt romances and is inspired daily by her own military-hero husband and four children. She hosts the *Stories to Love* podcast and is the *USA Today* bestselling author of *In a Book Club Far Away, Once Upon a Sunset, The Key to Happily Ever After,* and the Heart Resort and Journey to the Heart series.

TifMarcelo.com